WILD HEART MOUNTAIN: WILD RIDERS MC

BOOKS 1-3

SADIE KING

WILD RIDERS MC

BOOKS 1-3

If you love damaged ex-military heroes and curvy girl romance then you'll love the Wild Riders MC.

This group of ex-military bikers fall hard and fall first when they encounter the curvy women who heal their hearts.

Expect forced proximity, forbidden love, age gap, single moms and off limits love with OTT protector heroes who will do anything for the women they love.

This collection includes the first three novellas in the Wild Riders series plus bonus scenes.

Book 1 – Wild Ride

If a hot ex-military biker offered to give you anything you desired, what would you ask for?

A forced proximity, age gap instalove romance

featuring an OTT obsessed biker who falls hard and falls first.

Book 2 – Wild Hope – Bonus scene included

Why is forbidden love the sweetest?

A big brother's best friend forbidden love romance.

Book 3 – Wild Runaway – Bonus scene included

A single mom in danger and the ex-military biker who becomes her protector...

This reclusive protector hero becomes an insta-dad in this forced proximity, age gap, single mom romance.

Copyright © 2023 by Sadie King.

All rights reserved.

No part of this book may be reproduced in any form or by any electronic or mechanical means, including information storage and retrieval systems, without written permission from the author, except for the use of brief quotations in a book review.

Cover designed by Cormer Covers.

This is a work of fiction. Any resemblance to actual events, companies, locales or persons living or dead, are entirely coincidental.

Please respect the author's hard work and do the right thing.

www.authorsadieking.com

CONTENTS

WILD RIDE	1
WILD HOPE	83
WILD RUNAWAY	175
Wild Curves	277
Chapter One	279
Get your FREE Books	289
Books by Sadie King	291
About the Author	293

WILD RIDE

WILD RIDE

If an attractive ex-military biker offered to give you anything you desired, what would you ask for?

Danni

Mom always made the decisions for me: Go to college, get a good job in the city, find a nice man in a suit.

Instead, I've lost my job and I've lost my apartment. I'm single, I still have my v-card, *and* I'm wildly attracted to the bearded, tattooed biker who rescued me and my broken-down Caddy.

I've only ever done things to please Mom until I meet Colter.

He offers me a weekend of yes. One entire weekend where he will do whatever I ask of him.

It's a fun game at first, but as the weekend goes on, I

realize the only thing I want from him is one he's not prepared to give: his heart.

Colter

I don't do relationships. I have my MC club, my vintage bike collection, and my oversized dog. Women are trouble and best left alone.

But when I see Danni, stranded on the side of my mountain and looking like a pin-up straight out of the fifties, I can't resist. It's been a long time since I let a woman on the back of my bike. But Danni is one curvy exception.

She's spent too long pleasing others, and now it's my duty to please her.

As long as she knows it's just for the weekend…

Wild Ride is a forced proximity steamy instalove age gap romance featuring an ex-military mountain man biker and the curvy younger woman who steals his heart.

1
DANNI

The gear box shrieks as I shift into third and then down to second to take the hairpin corner with as much grace as a 1956 Cadillac Coupé de Ville on a narrow mountain road can.

Why the heck I thought driving my vintage car to the mountains was a good idea, I'll never know. I'll add it to the list of poor decisions I've made this year, which quite frankly is getting embarrassingly long and growing longer by the minute. If those rain clouds are anything to go by, I've booked a mountain retreat on the one summer weekend when it's going to rain.

The road evens out, and I take Gertie back to third. We're in fourth for one glorious moment before the next corner looms, and I'm shifting down through third and into second. My foot aches from pressing the clutch, and Mom's voice rings in my ears.

I didn't bring you up to change your own gears. Why didn't you get an automatic?

I'm shifting through to second when it happens. There's a clicking noise that I've been ignoring for the last several miles, ever since I started up the mountain road, and now it gets louder as I experience a momentary loss of power.

I steer Gertie around the corner, but there's a looseness about her that worries me. My Caddy shouldn't coast like that.

Then the puttering starts.

"Oh no. Come on, girl." I'm still twenty minutes out from my vacation cottage, and there's nothing but valley below and mountain above. "You can make this."

She can't. Gertie gives a final shudder before losing power. I manage to tuck her into the gravel at the side of the road as best I can before she dies completely.

"Not again."

I pull on the hand break, one of those old-fashioned stick ones, as steam wafts up from under the hood. At least, I hope it's steam. Steam I can deal with.

Gertie's been overheating ever since I spent an entire two months' wages to put down the deposit on her. I'll be paying off Gertie for the next five years, but the thrill of owning a piece of America's Golden Age was too good to pass up. Even if she is covered in rust and prone to overheating.

All I have to do is wait till she cools down and top off

the water. I carry a spare gallon in the trunk for just such occasions.

I get out of the car, and an acrid smell hits my nostrils. The distinctive smell of smoke. Smoke is a different story. Smoke is a problem I don't know how to fix.

Make sure you get roadside insurance. You'll need it with that thing.

Mom's words of encouragement pop into my head. It's the first thing she said when she saw the car, her arms folded across her chest in the way she does when I've disappointed her, which is often these days.

She couldn't understand why I spent so much on such an old car. I didn't try to explain the vintage aesthetic to her. I love anything from the fifties, and I've always wanted to travel across the States in a big old American car.

The irony of that is not lost on me. Now that I'm with said big ole American car, I've broken down on the side of a mountain, and I didn't get roadside insurance because I spent all my money on the car. Yup, living the dream.

I raise the hood and peer into the engine, just in case there's a big red button that says 'push this and the car will be fixed.'

Nope. Nothing like that. Just lots of grease-covered engine bits that all seem like they're in the right places to me.

Maybe there's someone at the vacation cabin who can

come out and fetch me. I check my phone. There are no bars, which means no service up here. Of course there's not. I'm stranded on the side of the road with a beautiful but useless car.

You should have got the Kia Hybrid like your sister.

"Shut up Mom."

2
COLTER

There is nothing in this world that comes close to the pure joy of the hum of your bike, the wind on your back, and the open road. Especially when your belly's full of a good steak and your hands are dirty with mechanic grease.

"Isn't that right, Daisy?"

My voice gets lost in the wind, but the body shifts behind me and a wet tongue slurps the side of my neck. I'm wearing a leather jacket and a biker's helmet, but Daisy still manages to find the one bit of exposed skin to give me a lick. My neck scrunches up at the contact.

"Ooh that tickles."

Daisy gives a bark and sits back in her seat.

I spent the morning working on one of my bikes and then had a late lunch with the guys at the bar. Now I'm riding home with my girl on the back. It looks like it's going to rain, but we should make it back in good time.

You get used to reading the weather when you live in the mountains.

I come around the corner, and there's a big old Caddy blocking the road. Lucky I'm taking it Friday-afternoon-easy, and there isn't another car coming the other way. I slow down to feast my eyes on the vintage vehicle.

It's a beauty, that's for sure. 1956 Series 62 Coupé de Ville. There's rust on the body and it could do with a paint job, but the curves on her are a thing of beauty.

Then I see the driver.

My bike pulls to a stop, sending gravel kicking up behind me. Daisy slides forward, her full weight slamming into my back before she scrambles to right herself.

She whines her displeasure, but my attention is taken by the beauty leaning against the driver's side of the Caddy.

She's wearing a cute polka dot dress with a high waist and a red band tied under her impressive breasts. The skirt billows out to fan around her knees, showing off her hourglass figure, and I don't mean a stick figure either. This woman is right out of the 1950s, her curves as pronounced as the Caddy she's leaning against.

Gloss stains her lips and her dark hair is pulled back with a hair band, causing stray tendrils to whip around her oval-shaped face.

She's the pin-up girl of my dreams. A Bettie Paige in the flesh, but much prettier.

The woman looks startled when I stop the bike and

reverse it to the side of the road so it's tucked in front of her car.

Her eyes are wide and anxious as she takes me in. I don't blame her. I'm wearing my Wild Riders MC leather jacket with the emblem emblazoned on the back. Even though there's nothing criminal about our motorcycle club--we're just a bunch of military veterans who love to ride--a man in a biker's patch on a big-ass motorbike could look intimidating to a lady on her own.

I give her my best smile to put her at ease.

"You got car trouble?"

Her gaze rakes over me, and I hope I stack up. Her suspicious look softens when she takes in Daisy. My oversized Mastiff gives us a mournful look and drops her head to her front paws.

The woman smiles, her expression softening, confirming that my dog is better with women than I am.

"There was smoke coming out of the hood, and I lost power. I don't know what it is."

It's a totally impractical car for these mountain roads is what it is. Everyone who lives here either drives a pickup or a motorbike. But I'm not going to tell her that.

"It's your lucky day."

She squints at me, suspicious again. "Why is that?"

She's chewing a piece of gum, and I have to shake myself to make sure I haven't time travelled back to the fifties.

"I'm a mechanic."

Her eyes widen. "Are you kidding me?"

"Nope."

She smiles with relief, and I wonder how long she's been here and consider how lucky I am that some other fucker didn't come along and find her first.

"Pop the hood and I'll take a look for you."

I'm a bike mechanic, but she doesn't need to know that. I know my way around car engines, and as it happens, 1950s engines too.

"I'm Colter."

I hold out a hand, and even though there are grease stains on my fingers she doesn't hesitate.

"I'm Danni."

Her fingernails have shiny red polish on them, and I want to keep that little hand in mine and find out all about Danni.

Warmth courses through my body as I clasp her hand in mine, not releasing the handshake.

Shit, it's been too long since I've been with a woman. I drop her hand quickly and turn to the car. And I'm not about to get involved with one now.

She opens the hood, and I move around to the front of the car. Danni hovers nearby, chewing her gum nervously.

The engine's original and it hasn't been maintained too well, not in the last few years at least. The whole thing could do with a fine tune, but her immediate problem is the intake valves. I don't tell her that straight away. I'm enjoying being near her too much.

"Where you from, Danni?"

"Charlotte."

I raise an eyebrow. She's a city girl. No wonder she's ill-equipped for the mountains. "You visiting someone?"

"I'm here for a vacation."

I bet there's a guy. Some lucky asshole who she's meeting.

"A retreat really. Just me."

Relief floods me, but she looks alarmed at what she's just said--admitting to a stranger that she's on her own.

"Don't worry, I'm harmless. Ask Daisy." Daisy gives a bark at her name and paws the seat, trying to get down. "You wait a little longer, honey. I don't want you loose on the roads."

Danni goes over to pat Daisy while I check over her car.

My big old attention craving Mastiff slobbers on Danni's hand and tries to lick her face. Danni laughs at Daisy's antics.

The sound of her laugh and the fact that it's because of my dog warms me up inside. Anyone who's kind to my dog is a good person.

I slam the hood down and wipe my hands on a rag I keep in my back pocket. Danni looks up expectantly.

"Your valves are worn out."

She winces. "That sounds bad."

"It's an easy fix. I can get you towed back to the shop."

She tugs on a strand of loose hair. I feel for this woman, breaking down in a strange place. "Thank you. How long till someone can come out?"

It's Friday afternoon, and I left the guys drinking at the Wild Taste Bar and Restaurant. On the off chance one of them is still sober enough to drive, and by the time I get home and make the call, it'll be longer than I want to leave a woman stranded on the side of a road, especially a pretty one.

"About a couple of hours."

Her face falls, and at that moment a grey cloud covers the sun.

"Okay, thanks. I'll wait in my car."

Her hand goes to the handle, and she pulls the door open. I can't leave her on the side of the road. Not with rain coming.

"Where are you staying. I'll drop you there?"

She looks at the bike and at Daisy, who's escaped her special seat and is now spread across the bike drooling on the leather.

"On that?"

Daisy lifts her head and gives me an unhappy whine as if she knows what I'm thinking. But she'll have to suck it up, because I've finally met a woman I want on the back of my bike.

"There's always room for one more."

3

DANNI

I'm wedged onto the back of a motorbike between a leather-clad giant of a man wearing an MC patch and an oversized and extra slobbery dog.

Every so often Daisy leans forward to lick my neck and grunt into my ear. I think that means she likes me. I only wish her owner liked me as much.

Colter is by far the hottest man I've ever met. He's big with broad shoulders and he should be intimidating, but the cheeky smile that peeps out from behind his well-maintained beard and the way his eyes crinkle when he laughs puts me at ease. Gentle giant comes to mind, although I've only known him for a few minutes.

Silver streaks his dark hair, and I think he must be at least ten years older than me. The biker jacket is like a red flame to my inner rebel, and underneath the jacket is a tight black t-shirt that lets me know he's packing some serious muscles.

His leather jacket sports a Wild Riders MC patch, and I can hear Mom's voice in my head.

You're not getting on the back of a bike with a man like that.

Oh yes I am, Mom. Yes I am.

The ride through the mountain roads is exhilarating. The wind whips my hair off my face, and I cling on to Colter as he expertly takes every bend in the road.

Too soon we're pulling into a gravel driveway with a sign that's hanging off the fence and reads 'Vacation Cabin.'

As Colter brings the bike to a stop, I squint at the cabin, trying to marry it with the images on the booking website.

"Is this the place?" He sounds as dubious as I feel.

The 'cabin' is a small shed with a wooden door that's rotted at the bottom. As I step onto the two-plank wide verandah, a squawking comes from the roof and a pair of swallows fly out through a hole in the rafters.

I pull up the details of the booking on my phone.

"One room cabin in idyllic setting. Rustic."

Colter snorts. "Rustic? The place is falling apart."

My heart sinks as I check out the cabin, because he's not wrong. The inside is worse than the outside if that's possible. The single bed looks lumpy, and the one light switch shows cobwebs in the corners and a thick layer of dust.

"You sure this is the right place?"

I read over the ad on the booking form. 'Rustic cabin at cut price rates. A base for your fishing trip or a hiking hut. No frills bed for the night.'

The ad basically told me, albeit in fancy language, that this place was run down. I stupidly booked it because it was 80% off.

"Yeah. This is the place."

My heart sinks. Of course this is where I would book to stay, because my whole life is one disaster after another and I can't even get it right when I try to escape to the mountains to sort said life out.

"You can't stay here."

I drop my backpack on the table. It's the only bit of luggage I could fit in Colter's saddle bag.

"It's not ideal, but it's just a bed for the night."

I try to be upbeat and take a seat on the bed. The bed springs squeak, and there's a scurrying noise. A giant rat bursts out from under the bed and scampers across the floor.

I scream like the city girl I am and jump on the bed, sending a wave of dust into the air.

Colter raises his eyebrows at me and holds out a hand.

"Come on. I'm getting you out of here."

I only hesitate for a second before I take his hand and let him lead me out of the cabin and into the fresh air.

"Is there anywhere else I can stay? A hotel or something?" I hate to think of the expense, but I'm not staying in a rat-infested cabin, that's for sure. And with my car broken down, I can't drive back home.

Colter squints at the sky. The clouds have gotten darker, and that rain will be here soon.

"I've got just the place."

We get on the back of his bike and I wedge myself between him and Daisy. The big dog rests her head on my shoulder and sighs heavily, as if she's the one with nowhere to spend the night.

Another ten minutes down the road and we pull into a gravel driveway that winds through a thicket of trees and opens up in front of a log cabin. This one's well maintained, and I breathe a sigh of relief. The verandah's wide and welcoming with two Cape Cod seats out front and a door that actually shuts. A string of fairy lights adorns the entryway, giving the place a welcome feel.

Colter slides off his bike then helps me down.

"Is this a B&B?" It looks too homely to be a hotel.

Colter gives me a slight smile that makes my insides flutter. "Not usually."

I'm about to ask what he means, but just then the rain finally arrives. And when it rains in the mountains, it really rains.

Thick drops fall out of the sky like bullets. We make a dash for the front porch, and I'm bowled out of the way by Daisy. I guess she doesn't like the rain because she's first to the door, whining to be let in.

Colter pulls out a key and unlocks the door and we tumble into the house, shaking the water off ourselves.

Wait a minute. If Colter's got a key...

"Do you live here?"

Colter slides his jacket off and hangs it on the coat rack by the door.

"This is my cabin. You can stay until your car is fixed."

My mouth drops open. "You can't be serious."

I can't stay in a stranger's cabin. And certainly not a stranger who's the Hottest Man I've Ever Met. My insides are quivering at the thought, and there's instant heat between my legs. My body's telling me yes, but luckily my brain knows this is a bad idea.

Colter puts his hands in the air. "Look, you don't know me. I get it. If you want to call someone, let them know where you are, I'll give you the address. You can also call the local police department. They'll vouch for me."

He seems sincere, but he's in a motorcycle club. He probably has the police department in his pocket. That's what MC clubs do, don't they?

Daisy chooses this moment to lick my hand and reminds me that anyone with a cute dog can't be that bad.

At that moment my phone buzzes, which is a relief. At least I've got signal again. It's Mom, obvs. Wanting a picture of the cabin and checking I made it okay.

I didn't make it okay, and I'm not going to send her a picture of the run down shed I was supposed to stay in. Mom would have a fit if she knew I was here with a strange man even contemplating spending the night. But

Mom isn't here, and for once I need to trust my own instincts.

Part of me is saying to get out of here, even if it means walking in the rain down the mountain to the last town I passed several miles back. But another part of me says Colter is safe. I'd be lying if I didn't admit that the thought of spending a night in his cabin is intriguing.

"That's a kind offer, but are you sure there's nowhere else I can go?"

He fixes me with an intense gaze that makes my cheeks and my core heat.

"Not in this weather."

The rain has turned to a downpour, and I get his point. But it's not just the rain. I want to be here. I want to spend the night in Colter's cabin. A thought occurs to me.

"Will your wife be okay with this…?"

His eyebrow raises slightly, and he smiles like he's pleased at my question. Heat rises up my neck and I glance away, not wanting him to see me blushing. It shouldn't matter to me if he has a wife, but damn it, I'm hanging on his answer.

"I'm not married."

His eyes twinkle as he says it, and I get the feeling he's enjoying my discomfort. I try not to let my relief show, while inside my chest is fluttering. The Hottest Man I've Ever Met is single, and I'm in his cabin for the night. Although it occurs to me that he still might have a girlfriend, but asking him that now might make him think I'm interested.

"I don't want to put you out," I say, but he knows I'm wavering.

"You're not putting me out, Danni. It's nice to have you here."

He gives me a soft smile that makes my core tighten. Then he turns and walks away.

"Come. I'll show you around."

I snap a quick picture of the living room showing the fireplace and wolfskin rug and send it to Mom.

Got here safe, place is great.

If only she knew…

4
COLTER

Danni is spread out on the couch in front of the fireplace. I couldn't fit her suitcase on the bike, so she had to leave most of her clothes in her car. Her dress got soaked in the sudden downpour, and while it dries she's wearing one of my sweaters. It's too big on her and the bagginess hides her curves, but it's sexy as hell seeing her in my clothes.

So sexy I have to adjust my pants to hide the semi I've had ever since she slid onto the back of my bike, her body pressed up against mine thanks to Daisy taking up most the space back there.

It's been a long time since I had a woman on the back of my bike, and I'd forgotten how good it feels. How soft her thighs were as they bumped up against me, how her breasts pressed into my back when we leaned into the corners.

When we got to the sorry excuse for a rental cabin she was supposed to stay in, I couldn't believe my luck. There was no way I was letting her stay in a place like that. And no way I was taking her anywhere else but here.

I could have told her about the Blue Emerald Lodge or the hotel in Hope or any number of B&Bs in Wild, the closest town. But I didn't, God help me. I pretended like the only decent thing to do was to take her back to my cabin for the night.

There's nothing decent about my intentions for getting her here. I don't do relationships, but when a curvy brunette comes my way, I might just do a weekend of fun.

"You like mushrooms?"

Danni looks up from her phone where she's been scrolling all afternoon. Her mouth is parted, making her lips seem bigger. I've never seen such a kissable mouth. I bet she tastes like bubble gum and strawberries or whatever lip gloss she's got on.

"They're real mountain mushrooms, picked wild."

"Sounds good. Do you need a hand?"

It's about the third time she's asked me, and her anxious expression makes me want to find something for her to do. But the truth is I like having someone to cook for.

It's been me and Daisy up here alone since I got back from the military five years ago. I swore off women a long time ago, and usually Daisy, my bikes, and the MC are all I need. But a man could get used to having someone like Danni lounging on his couch.

"You could pour the wine."

She jumps up from the couch and tosses her phone aside. It immediately buzzes, but she ignores it.

"Your boyfriend?"

I try to keep my voice casual, but a sharp pang of jealousy pierces my chest.

"No. My mom."

They must be close if that's who she's been texting all afternoon. "So you don't have a boyfriend?"

"No."

I hand her a bottle of red and an opener.

"You said you're not married; do you have a girlfriend?"

She asked earlier about a wife, and it's not lost on me that she's now clarifying the situation.

"It's just me and Daisy." The big dog lifts her head at the sound of her name then goes back to sleeping by the fire.

I'm more than a little happy that Danni asked me my relationship status. But if she's interested, I need to clarify something from the start.

"I don't do relationships."

Danni sloshes the wine into the glasses, and some of it goes over the side and onto the kitchen counter.

"You don't?"

She seems a little disappointed, and that causes a pang

in my chest. I shake the thought off and grab a dishcloth to mop up the wine.

"Nope."

I don't want to go into the specifics of why I don't believe in love, so I change the subject.

"What brings you to the mountains?"

Danni winces and looks away. "It's a long story."

By this time the pasta sauce is ready, and I grab two bowls to dish it up.

"We've got all night."

I take the bowls over to the table, and Danni follows with the wine. She takes a delicate sip, leaving a smear of lip gloss on the glass.

"I wanted to get away for a few days."

"Get away from what?"

She eats slowly, taking her time to answer the question.

"My whole life, really."

I sit back and look at her. She's got to be in her early twenties. I wonder what could have happened to get her so down.

"What are you running from?"

She shrugs. "It's nothing serious. No one's chasing me or anything. It's just that my life is a mess. *I'm* a mess. You know?"

"You don't look like a mess to me."

She looks far from a mess. The opposite of a mess. She looks delicious and sexy and like I want to gobble her right up. But there is a sadness about Danni. Her smile never quite reaches her eyes.

"I lost my job," she blurts out. "And my apartment."

Well, that explains it. I take a bite of pasta, waiting for her to tell me more.

"I even lost my cat. Darn thing went off just when the movers arrived, and I called her for ages but she didn't come back…"

She sniffs and wipes a tear carefully from her eye with the back of her finger.

"I'm sorry about your cat."

"Thanks." Her look is sheepish. "Actually, I think the neighbors had been feeding her for a while. She'll be fine. Cats always are."

"How'd you lose your job?"

"I took a voluntary buyout." She winces when she says it like I might judge her. But hell, I'm not here to judge, just to listen. "I hated working for a bank, so when they asked for volunteers to take a buyout, I said I'd go. But I'd only been there a few months, so the payout wasn't good."

She trails off and raises the wine glass to her lips. This time she takes a big gulp.

"Your mom wouldn't approve?"

Danni gives me a look. "That's an understatement." She takes another gulp of wine, and I wait for her to continue.

"Mom is… particular."

"Particular?" I raise my eyebrows, trying to understand what she's telling me.

"She has this idea of what my life should be like, and I've always followed it. I went to college, I did an MBA like she wanted me to, I got a job in the city for a banking firm because I knew it would make her happy. But I hated it."

Her shoulders slump like she's got the weight of the world on them.

"Can't you do what you want to do?"

"Sometimes. Like I bought that totally impractical car because I loved it, but now it's broken down, so…" She shrugs. "Whenever I do something to please myself, it ends up going wrong anyway…"

She takes another gulp of wine and looks away. I try to imagine what it must be like trying to please someone else.

"That doesn't sound fair."

"The worst thing is that my sister does everything Mom wants, and she does it effortlessly. She got an economics degree, she works for one of the big banks in the city, she's engaged to a banker. My sister is living the perfect life, and here I am, no job, no apartment, no boyfriend…"

She trails off. "Sometimes I think Mom knows best and I feel bad for wanting things for myself, and sometimes I get so guilty because I'm not doing what Mom wants. She gave up so much for us kids. And I'm a terrible daughter because I can't make her proud."

That's a lot to put on someone, but I keep my thoughts to myself. I don't want to diss her mom, but it sounds like she's putting her daughter under a lot of stress.

"How old are you, Danni?"

"I'm twenty-three."

I was in Iraq when I was twenty-three, following my own dreams. It's what you should do when you're young.

"What if you did what you wanted to do for a change?"

She raises her gaze to meet mine. Her long eyelashes glisten with the hint of tears. "I wish it was that easy."

"It can be."

She shakes her head. "You don't understand my mother. She's…forceful."

"Well, she's not here."

Danni licks the wine off her lips, and my gaze darts to her mouth. A wicked idea is starting to form, and I wonder if I can get her to go along with it.

"For one weekend, why don't you do exactly what you want to do without trying to please anyone else? Just do what Danni wants."

Her brows knit together like she doesn't understand the concept. "Like, whatever I want?"

"Why not? You're on vacation. I'll even help you."

"How will you do that?"

"You request something, and I'll go out of my way to make it happen."

Her eyes widen as she thinks about it, and my dick

hardens. I'm a bad man. There's only one thing I hope Danni wants.

"So let me get this straight. If there's something I want this weekend, something I want to do and it's within your power to do so, you'll help me do it?"

I lick my lips, imagining Danni down on all fours asking me to fuck her.

"Anything you want. A weekend of yes."

She sits back in her chair, her eyes never leaving mine. Her manicured finger trails around the edge of the wine glass.

"A weekend of yes? How does that work?"

I lean forward, my eyes darting to her lips that I'm aching to kiss.

"You ask me for something, anything you want, and I say yes."

Her pupils widen. It's an indecent offer, and I have no idea what I'm doing. I've never said this to a woman before. I don't know what game I'm playing, but I want Danni to ask me to do bad things to her. I'm prepared for whatever she asks. I'll make her scream my name as I make her come over and over again.

"Okay." Her voice comes out as a whisper, and a slow smile spreads across her face as she comes around to the idea.

"So, what do you want to do Danni?" My voice is husky, and my cock's as hard as stone.

"I want to play chess."

It's not what I was hoping she'd say.

"I saw the carved set by the fireplace. I used to play with my dad before he left…" Her eyes flicker with uncertainty. "I mean, if you want a game, that is."

"Whatever you want. I'm here to help you forget about your mom's wishes and focus on yours. And if you want to play chess, that's what we'll do."

She grins, and it's the first time her eyes light up too.

"I want to play chess."

"Then let's get the board out."

My dick will have to wait.

5
DANNI

I wake to the sound of birdsong and the smell of bacon. The sheets on this bed are luxurious and I stretch lazily, enjoying the heaviness in my bones from a night of really good sleep. The rainstorm has passed, and sunlight peeps in from behind the curtains.

Last night we played chess by the fire. It was my first time playing since I was a kid, and I'm sure Colter was going easy on me. He won four games and I won one, and even then I don't think he was playing his best.

We talked as we played, and I got to know more about my handsome rescuer. Like that he was in the military, he's a bike mechanic, and the MC he's a part of is a group of ex-military guys who love to ride. Nothing illegal he assures me, which goes to show how much I know about motorcycle clubs.

He put me to bed in the spare room, which was slightly disappointing but the gentlemanly thing to do. It took me ages to get to sleep because I was thinking about Colter down the hall and wondering what he'd do if I snuck out of bed and slipped in beside him.

But that's not the type of girl Mom raised me to be, even if my body goes into overdrive whenever I gaze into his dark eyes.

I find Colter in the kitchen with bacon sizzling on the stove top.

He goes still when he sees me, and his eyes widen. Most of my clothes are still in the suitcase in the trunk of my beautiful but useless car, so I slept in a flannel shirt he leant me.

It's more of a dress on me and falls almost to my knees. That's where Colter's eyes dart, to the line of skin that's poking out where the shirt rides up on the sides of my thighs.

My skin prickles under his gaze and heat spreads up my thighs, making my core clench tight. I squirm uncomfortably, hoping he doesn't notice the reaction I'm having to his gaze. If his eyes on me can cause my body to heat this much, I can only imagine what the feel of his touch would do.

"Morning." Colter clears his throat and drags his gaze away from my thighs. "You sleep okay?"

I stretch lazily, then realize that makes the shirt ride up. I drop my arms and tug on the hem, but not before his gaze darts back to my legs. He swallows hard, and desire flashes across his face.

I can't say I mind the look he's giving me. My legs go

wobbly, and I slide onto a kitchen stool before they give out.

"Like a log," I lie, But I'm not going to tell him I lay awake thinking about him half the night. "It's so peaceful here. You?"

Colter's gaze finds mine. "I was restless."

My cheeks flush. Was he restless because of me? I'm sure he senses this attraction too, but he made it clear that he doesn't want a relationship. Then he went and made that tantalizing offer to do whatever I want this weekend. My thoughts immediately went dirty, thinking about asking him to touch me down there. But I don't have much experience with men, and I'm not sure what I'd ask for.

Colter holds up a tray of eggs.

"How do you like 'em? Fried, scrambled, or poached?"

I love that he's asking, but I don't want to put him out any more than I am already.

"However you're having them."

Colter shakes his head slowly, making a tutting sound. "That's not how this works, Danni. It's your weekend, remember? You ask for everything exactly how you want it."

The words make my core turn liquid even though he's only talking about eggs. It felt fun in the moment and after a glass of wine to agree to a weekend of yes, as he put it, but he can't mean to go through with it, can he?

"No really, I don't want to be a nuisance."

He gives me a disapproving look, and my insides

shrink. It's the kind of look Mom gives me when I give her the wrong answer.

Colter stalks over to me until he's so close I can smell his pine scent and musky body wash.

"This weekend is about you, Danni, living exactly how you want. So tell me, how do you want your eggs?"

It's such a simple question, but no one has ever asked me that before. Mom always said I should eat eggs poached because that's the healthiest way. She disapproved of the curves that remained stubbornly on my body no matter what diet she tried to put me on.

I think about it for way longer than a question about how you want your eggs should warrant.

"Fried, please. Two eggs."

I say it quietly, wondering if he's going to think I'm unhealthy for wanting fried eggs and greedy for wanting two of them. But after two glasses of wine last night, I need some grease. Colter only nods his approval and turns back to the pan.

A few minutes later, I'm biting into a bacon and fried egg sandwich with ketchup and egg yolk running down my chin. It's messy, it's inelegant, and it's the most delicious breakfast I've ever tasted.

"Mmmm." A moan escapes me as I bite into the eggy goodness. Colter's eyes widen as he watches me eat. I should probably be embarrassed about the way I'm stuffing my face, but today's all about me, right?

"This is good," I say between mouthfuls. "Thank you."

He leans forward and wipes yolk from the corner of

my mouth. The touch makes me shiver deliciously, and for a moment I think he's going to kiss my egg-stained lips, but he sits back instead.

"What would you like to do today?"

I chew my last bite thoughtfully.

"Is there a post office? I promised Mom I'd send her a card. Or a really good view so I can post some pictures for Mom..."

I trail off at the way Colter's looking at me.

"But what do *you* want to do, Danni? Not for your mom, but for *you*?"

His words bring me up short. I never realized how much of what I do is for her. It's not Mom's fault. She raised me and my sister on her own, working two jobs so she could send us to college. She wants a better life for us than she had, and now that we've both left home she's lonely.

I decide to take a few pics from whatever we end up doing and sending them to her tonight. But until then, I won't think about Mom for the rest of the day.

But what do I want to do. What does Danni Malone want to do today?

I watch Colter across the table. By the looks he's been giving me, I'm sure he's as attracted to me as I am to him. What I really want to do is kiss his smiling lips and find out if his beard scratches when it's between my legs.

I squeeze my thighs together at the thought. If only he knew what I was thinking. Instead, I say the next best thing I'd like to do.

"Is there good hiking around here?"

Colter nods his approval, and I'm pleased I've hit on something he enjoys too. "The best."

"Where there's no people. I don't want to see people today."

A grin spreads across his face.

"As you wish."

"Wait, did you just quote *The Princess Bride* at me?"

Colter chuckles. "One of my favorite all time movies."

I guffaw imagining this big tough biker guy watching *The Princess Bride.*

"Can we watch it later?"

Colter stands up to clear the plates. As he reaches for mine, he leans forward so his lips whisper in my ear.

"As you wish, Princess."

Oh boy. The warmth from his lips caresses my skin and sends heat skittering over my body. I'm having a weekend of doing whatever I want, and I think what I want to do is Colter.

6
COLTER

I've changed out my full leather jacket for the vest with the cut-off sleeves that has the Wild Riders cut on the back. But I'm still sweating like a waterfall as we hike the last stretch of my favorite trail.

Danni's panting behind me, and the way her chest heaves up and down with the exertion is driving me nuts. I've had a hard-on for this woman ever since I found her on the side of my mountain. But seeing her in cutoff jeans and a tank top with perspiration beading on her chest is something else.

My dick pushes uncomfortably against my jeans, and if she keeps making those panting noises, I might just lose it in my boxers like a teenager.

The trail crests the hill and evens out to a flat area. I take a side path that's hidden between the pine trees and undergrowth and leads to my favorite spot. The path winds through scrub before opening out to a rocky pool at the base of a small waterfall.

"You want to rest here?"

Danni nods gratefully as she leans against an enormous boulder. I shrug off the backpack and hand her a water bottle. She tilts her neck back and guzzles the water, letting some of it trickle down her throat.

Christ. My cock twitches. I fight an urge to run my tongue up her throat and lap up every bead of water and sweat. I have to turn away to stop myself from acting on my instincts. Today is supposed to be about her wants, not mine.

Danni finishes her drink, and as she lowers the water bottle, she takes in her surroundings for the first time. Her eyes widen at the view.

This rocky pool is Wild Heart Mountain's best kept secret. The pool is nestled among a thicket of trees that shield it from the main path. The waterfall is only a trickle in summer, making it less visited than some of the bigger ones. And the other edge of the rocky pool looks out over the tree-covered valley.

The town of Wild is far below, barely a blip amongst a sea of green. This is the lesser populated part of the mountain dominated by the tall pines grown commercially to supply the Wild Sawmill. Most residents live over on the other side of the mountain near Hope. The Wild side of Wild Heart Mountain is, well, wilder. An untamed wilderness free of resorts and ski hills and the tourists that come with them.

"It's beautiful."

My eyes are still on Danni. "Sure is."

She glances at me quickly, and I don't look away. I can't hide my attraction to her. She fans herself and looks longingly at the water.

"I wish I could jump in and cool off."

"Why don't you?"

She frowns at me as if I've grown two heads. "I didn't bring my swimsuit."

"Who needs a swimsuit?"

Her mouth pops open as she gets my meaning. "You mean...skinny dip?"

I sure as hell do.

I keep eye contact with her as I slide off my vest and peel off the t-shirt underneath. My muscles are firm from the labor I do around the cabin, and I catch Danni staring at them. Her gaze is hungry, and I wish she'd come over here and take a bite.

"You can't be serious?" She looks alarmed even as her gaze rakes over my body.

She's a city girl all right and obviously used to doing the right thing. I'm dying for her to cast off her inhibitions and let herself free.

"Why not? You want to go for a swim, what's stopping you? It's your day, remember Danni? Your choice."

She glances around furtively. "What if someone comes along?"

I shrug. "Who cares. You want to cool off, or you want to worry about what strangers think?"

I turn around before I slide my jeans off so she doesn't see my dick causing a tent in my underwear. The water is cool on my overheated skin as I step into the pool. I duck my head as I push off from the side, letting the water swirl over me.

When I come up, Danni's standing by the far side of the pool looking uncertain.

"It's refreshing."

"Refreshing. That means freezing cold, right?"

I shake my head. "The sun's warmed it up. It's nice."

I turn away, hoping the privacy will give her the confidence she needs. I'm not wrong. The sound of clothes sliding off her body makes my dick convulse, and a few moments later I hear her slip into the pool.

When I turn around, only her head and shoulders are visible. A bright pink bra strap with lace details runs over her shoulder, and her breasts bob just below the surface. So tantalizing.

"See, not cold."

"It's lovely." She paddles around the pool before moving to the edge that looks out over the valley. She rests her elbows on the edge of the pool and turns back toward me.

"What do you like most about living on the mountain?"

I tread water in the middle of the pool, loving the sight of the sunlight bouncing off her hair.

"The privacy."

"Oh." Her face falls. "Sorry, you've been so kind to me

and here I am taking up your day. You probably want to be left alone."

"That's not what I meant."

I swim over to her before she can exit the pool and plant my hands on the rocks to either side of her.

"I like showing you around."

We're so close our noses are almost touching. She smells like the strawberry lip gloss she's always got smeared on her plump lips.

Her eyes dart to my lips, and I know she wants me to kiss her. But we're playing a game, and I want to make her ask.

"What do you want, Danni?"

My voice comes out husky with desire. A ripple of current makes me lose my footing and my body bumps into her, causing my dick to graze her stomach.

She gasps and her eyes go wide, desire pooling in their depths.

"Tell me what you want, and I'll give it to you."

She licks her lips. "I want to kiss you."

Her voice is breathless and needy, and she bites her lower lip as if I might refuse.

"As you wish."

I don't give her any old kiss. This thing has been building between us ever since I picked her up on the side of the mountain. When I press my mouth to hers, it's slow. Her lips part, and we explore each other. My tongue darts into her mouth and I taste her strawberry lip gloss, sticky on my lips.

When we come up for air, her eyes are hooded with desire.

My hand hovers in the water, the current pushing my knuckles so they brush up against her breast.

"What do you want, Princess?"

"I don't know."

I let my finger graze her nipple, and she takes in a sharp intake of breath.

"Tell me what you want."

She hesitates, worrying her bottom lip. "I want you to touch me."

"You want to be touched?"

My fingers trail down her throat, brushing her neck as she tilts it back.

"Yes," she whispers.

"Tell me where. Where do you want to be touched?"

"My…"

"Your neck?"

My fingers trail behind her ear, making her shudder as I find her erogenous zone.

"Touch my…"

She can't find the words, and her face is exquisite torture. I'm not going to make it easy for her. I like the sound of the need in her voice too much.

"Your shoulder?" My hands run over her shoulders and I slip my finger under one of the pink bra straps, letting it slide off her shoulder and down her arm. My fingertips trail over the exposed pale skin of the well of her chest.

"Touch my…"

I love the fact that my girl is too shy to say the words. I'll give her a little bit, but she has to ask for what she really wants.

"Touch your breasts?"

As I say it, my hand slides under her bra. Danni gasps as I graze her nipple. It pebbles under my touch, and I roll the hard peak around on my fingertips.

"You like that, Princess?"

"Yes," she gasps.

I explore her breasts as I kiss her neck and lips. She squirms against me, our bodies bumping against each other in the water.

"Is there something else you want me to touch?"

"Yes," she gasps.

"Say it, Princess. Ask for it like a good girl."

Her eyes flicker open, and the look she gives me is pure lust. Holy fuck, I think I've hit on something.

"Are you going to be a good girl for me?"

She nods vigorously. "Yes, Colter. I am."

Well shit. My girl likes to be praised.

"Then tell me what you want like a good girl."

"I want you to touch…"

She trails off again and I slide my hand up her thigh, enjoying the way she leans into the touch, shuddering against me.

"Ask for it, Danni. What do you want?"

"I want you to touch my… pussy."

There it is. The breathless way she says it has precum squirting out of me. I'm so hard for this woman I might lose it.

"Good girl."

As I praise her, my hand slides over the wet gusset of her panties. Even in the water, I feel her heat. She moans at my touch. It's good, but I want to give her more.

My thumbs hook over her panties, and I slide them off her legs. She gasps in surprise.

"You want me to stop?"

Danni shakes her head. "No."

"Good, because this is your day, Princess. I'm going to give you everything you need."

I slide her panties off her feet and chuck them on the rock behind her.

My hands grip her hips and I stroke her thighs, making my way back to her sweet hot spot.

She bites her lower lip, and I know that look now. There's something she wants but is too afraid to ask for.

"What do you want, Princess?"

She lowers her eyes, embarrassed. I let my palm slide between her legs, loving the way her curly hair feels so soft in the water.

She gasps at the contact as my fingers slide between her folds.

"I want…" She looks at me shyly. "I want you to… to kiss me down there."

Well fuck, she read my mind. But I'm not letting her get away that easy.

"Say it, Princess. Say the exact words like a good girl."

As I speak, my thumb brushes her clit, and her body convulses like a bolt of electricity has gone through it. My girl's a live wire, and I can't wait to have her humming on my tongue.

"I want you to kiss my pussy."

A grin spreads across my face.

"Good girl."

There's a ledge under the water, and I secure my feet there. Then, with my hands around her hips, I lift her out of the water.

Her hands rest on my shoulders as I sit her on the rock ledge before me. Water drips off her thighs as I run my hands over them and gently pry them apart. She opens up for me, exposing her beautiful pink pussy.

For a moment I can't breathe. Her pink folds drip with water and glisten with her own wetness. Her pearl peeks out shyly, invitingly. She's beautiful, stunning, and in this moment, all mine.

I kiss her thighs, moving slowly up her legs, enjoying her whimpering noises as my beard scraps against her soft skin. Her thighs part, and I pull her forward until I fit snugly between her legs. When I get to her core, the heat emanating off her intensifies as I brush my lips across her pink folds, planting a kiss on her most sensitive area as requested.

She gasps and grips my shoulders tight.

"You want me to just kiss it, or you want me to lick your pussy?"

She squirms, shuffling herself to get closer to me, her

inhibitions starting to fall away as she presses her pussy to my mouth.

"Lick it, Colter," she pants. "Lick my pussy."

"As you wish."

My tongue dips to her sticky sweet folds. I taste her, lapping her up hungrily. She's sweet and fresh, her taste mingling with the mountain river. I lap at her, licking and sucking slowly, enjoying my feast while the sun beats down on the both of us.

My arm hooks her thigh and I sling one leg over my shoulder, opening her up wide. She gasps and moans my name, and it's the sexiest sound I've ever heard.

My finger slides into her as my tongue laps her up.

Danni's moans mingle with the trickle of the waterfall and the birdsong. Her sweet scent gets more potent with her arousal and fills my nostrils, making my dick as hard as the rock she's sitting on. But my focus is all on Danni. On building her up to a release that she so obviously needs.

Her pussy's so tight that it pulls on my fingers as I pump her hard. Her hands tangle in my hair, pulling my head toward her. Then her body stiffens and she screams my name as she comes, sending a flock of birds cawing into the air.

Her thighs tighten around me and I cling on, pressing my mouth to her core until her body slackens.

She gives a gentle sigh, but I'm not done with her yet. I flick my tongue against her, and she gasps. It's all the encouragement I need. I don't make her ask for the second orgasm. I could do this all day, pulling orgasms out of my girl.

I give her three more until her body is spent. Only once she sags back against the rocks do I release her thighs and wipe her juices out of my beard.

Danni leans back on the rocks, her thighs splayed open with pussy juice trailing down them. It's a beautiful sight, and one I could get used to. I splash water on her thighs, washing her down. She smiles at me, a lazy satisfied smile that goes straight to my heart.

Maybe this old mountain man could get used to having a woman around after all. I told her it was just for the weekend, but now that I've had a taste, I'm not sure if that's still what I want.

I was hurt once before, and I swore I'd never let a woman get close. But when I look at Danni basking in the sun, my heart squeezes painfully. I've got a weekend with her, but will that be enough?

7
DANNI

The hike down the mountain is a slower pace than the hike up. Probably because my legs are wobbly from the multiple orgasms Colter gave me. We hold hands the whole way down the trail, and I can't get the stupid grin off my face.

It's just for the weekend, but man, a girl could get used to this.

"What do you want to do now, Princess?"

The nickname makes me glow with pleasure. I feel like a Princess today and he's my willing servant, wanting nothing more than to do as I wish. An image flashes into my brain of Colter's head between my thighs and his hot mouth on my pussy. My core tightens, and I'm about to say we should go back to his place for more orgasms, but I can't quite form the words. It's not fair to ask him to sexually pleasure me all day, even though I'm pretty sure he enjoyed it as much as I did. Besides, if I have even one more orgasm right now, my whole body might turn to jelly.

"I want to see your vintage bikes."

Colter gives a surprised smile, and I can tell he's pleased. Even though he said this weekend is all about me, what I want to do is find out all about him. He mentioned last night that he has a bike collection, and I love anything vintage.

"As you wish."

A little while later we're back at Colter's place, and he slides open the rustic-looking garage door of a shed behind the cabin. The inside is anything but rustic.

This place is pristinely clean. Ten different bikes sit proudly in neat rows, the chrome polished to a high sheen on every single one of them.

The first in the row is a Harley that looks like it's from the 1940s. I run my fingertips along the vibrant turquoise casing, loving the smooth glossy texture.

"It's beautiful." As beautiful as my old Caddy but better preserved. "Does she still run?"

Colter grabs two vintage style helmets off a rack.

"You want to find out?"

I clap my hands together in excitement and do a little excited jump that makes Colter laugh. I love American vintage from the golden era, and this bike is a beauty.

The seat is smaller than his other bike I was on yesterday, and even with no Daisy behind me, I'm pushed right up against Colter's back. His touch reminds me of the intimacy we just shared, and a blush creeps up my neck as my body heats.

Colter starts the engine and it hums all the way up my thighs, making my core vibrate.

He pulls her out onto the mountain road, and this ride is exquisite torture. I'm humming inside, and there's no way to press my thighs together. With the angle I'm sitting at and my legs spread apart, the vibrations of the vintage engine have my panties wet and my core zinging.

By the time Colter takes a dirt road and pulls to a stop in a clearing, I'm horny as heck. I don't know if it's the fresh air, or the man, or the vibrations of the bike. But when Colter rests his foot on the ground and asks me over his shoulder what I want to do now, I bite my lower lip, still too embarrassed to ask for the release I crave.

A slow grin spreads over his face.

"As you wish."

I don't even need to say anything. Colter swivels around in the seat, changing positions so we're facing each other.

He keeps the engine running as his hand slides up my skirt. I'm so sensitive to any touch that his fingertips on my thighs have me gasping for air. And when he reaches my panties and strokes me through the fabric, I almost come undone.

"You're already wet."

"What can I say, I love bikes."

He chuckles.

"Good girl."

I whimper at the praise as his finger slides inside me. With his deft hands and the hum underneath me, I'm a ball of nerves ready to explode.

Colter rests his other hand on my shoulder and pulls me forward so my pussy's pressed to the seat of the bike where the vibrations are coming from.

"Colter…" My voice is a needy whine that I hardly recognize. "I'm not gonna last."

"Good. Come for me like the horny good girl you are."

Oh wow. His praise will be my undoing. I want to please him. I've been brought up my whole life to please, and now as he encourages me, I rock back and forth on his hand. He helps the motion, pulling me forward and back so I'm rocking into his palm as the bike vibrates under me.

The sensations reverberate throughout my body, and it doesn't take long for the orgasm to claim me.

"Colter!"

I scream his name as my pussy clenches around his fingers. The vibrations carry the orgasm down my legs to the tips of my toes and out to my fingertips and the ends of my hair. I feel the orgasm *everywhere* as a powerful force that releases all the tension I never knew I was carrying.

It's the most intense sensation I've ever experienced, and when I open my eyes, Colter's staring at me with unconcealed desire.

"God, you're beautiful when you come."

It's obvious he's got a hard-on, and while I love that he makes me feel like a Princess with all this attention, it's not really fair. I want to make him feel as good as I do.

My hands fumble with his belt buckle as I slide off the bike.

"What are you doing?"

"It's your turn."

Colter captures my hands, stopping them before I can reach his dick.

"This weekend is about you, Danni. You only have to do what you want."

My gaze meets his. "I want to make you feel good, Colter. I want to put your big cock in my mouth and suck it."

He groans at my dirty words, as surprised by them as I am. I've never spoken like that before. But it feels good and dirty. With Colter, I can let my inhibitions go.

"As you wish." His voice comes out choked. And I love that I have this effect on him.

I sink to my knees as Colter swings his leg over the side of the bike.

He leans against the bike as I pull his dick out of his jeans. I gasp in surprise, and panic takes hold. It's so big. A huge beast that's hard and purple with a bead of cum dripping off the end.

"Are they all this big?"

My alarmed eyes meet his, but Colter only smiles.

"Is this the first dick you've seen, Princess?"

Colter grabs himself around the base of the shaft and slides his hand up his glorious length. I'm mesmerized by the action.

"The first in real life."

His gaze flickers and he groans, a guttural sound that makes my pussy hum.

I never had much time for dating, and it wasn't worth it to see Mom's disappointment in any guy that I was remotely interested in. I gave up on men long ago. But here, with Colter, in the middle of a quiet forest, I'm rethinking my life choices.

I didn't know it would feel so powerful to make a man groan the way he does. I didn't know it would feel so good to have a man look at you with desire in his eyes. More than desire. With barefaced need.

"Are you a virgin, Danni?"

I tear my eyes away from his beast, and my gaze meets his. "I've never been with a man before."

He takes in a sharp intake of breath. "Good girl."

The praise goes straight to my heart, and I sit up a little straighter.

"I've never done this before either."

My hand reaches tentatively for his cock, and I wrap my fingers around it. My hand's not quite big enough for his girth. I wrap my other hand around to fill the gap and slide both hands up and down his sticky shaft.

"That's it. Just like that."

I love the praise that he's giving me. It makes me want

to do better. I've spent my life pleasing people, and now I want to please Colter.

Parting my lips, I press a kiss to the tip of his cock. It tastes salty and sweet, and I lick the cum off the tip.

Colter groans again, so I must be doing something right.

With new confidence, I slide his cock into my mouth. My mouth stretches for him, and I gag as he hits the back of my throat.

"Just take it easy, and when you're ready, open your throat."

I love that he's giving me directions. I do as he says, sucking and licking and exploring his cock. It's messy; I slobber everywhere and my teeth scrape his skin. But by the noises he's making, I think he likes it.

My knees scrape on the pine needles on the ground, sending pricks of pain up my thighs. His hands wrap around my head and he pulls me toward him, so I take in his whole shaft. I do as he says and open my throat as his cock slams into me.

"Good girl, Danni. You're good at sucking my cock."

Heat pools between my legs. With one hand on his cock, I reach my other hand into my panties. My pussy is sticky and hot, and I rub myself as I lick and suck on Colter's delicious cock. He pulls me up and down his shaft, telling what a good girl I am. The words make me insanely turned on. My own orgasm is building, but I want to please him first.

Colter pauses. "I'm going to cum." He tries to pull out, and I grip his cock with my lips and suck hard.

"You want me to cum in your mouth?" I nod. "Is that what my good girl wants?"

I moan at the words. Yes. It's what I want. I want to please him; I want to do whatever he needs me to do.

My sucking gets harder as I sense him getting closer.

"Good girl, Danni. Make me cum like a good girl."

The pressure builds in my core until I explode. At the same time, his cock thickens and hot cum lashes the back of my throat in thick ropes. It startles me as my mouth fills with his sticky liquid.

"Take my cum, Danni. Swallow it like a good Princess."

I do as I'm told, swallowing it all down, loving the way it burns my throat.

"Good girl, Danni."

Colter pats the top of my head, and I beam up at him as I slide his cock out of my mouth. I've never done that before, but for Colter, I'll get on my knees and be his good girl any day.

This is supposed to be my weekend to discover what I like to do. And what I like to do is get on my knees and suck Colter's cock.

If only there was a way to make it last longer than the weekend.

8
COLTER

For dinner I make Danni homemade pizza with extra cheese. I love having someone to cook for and we take our time, preparing the meal together and talking late into the night. The more time I spend with Danni, the more I question my insistence on it just being a weekend thing.

Danni is easy to talk to and quick to laugh, and she drives my body wild with her curves.

We fool around in bed and in the morning too. I can't get enough of pleasuring her, and the way her inexperienced hands fumble over my cock has me coming hard into her palm.

We spend a lazy morning in bed before taking one of the vintage bikes out for a spin. This time it's the 1940s Chopper, with a low seat and high handlebars. I strap Daisy's seat to the back. She was annoyed we didn't take her yesterday, giving me her sad puppy dog face, so today she rides with us.

Danni's car is being repaired at the mechanic's shop owned by the club. We have a compound on the main mountain road that we've filled with club-owned business.

There's a repair shop and the Wild Taste Brewery which makes craft beer with fresh mountain water. Out front is Wild Taste Bar and Restaurant where you can sample the beer from the brewery and enjoy a good hearty meal.

This is where I take Danni for lunch. I want her to see my world, my club, and the places I hang out.

"This is your clubhouse?"

Danni takes in the bike paraphernalia adorning the walls with wide eyes and a grin on her face. I like making her smile, and so far, all the parts of me I've shown her have made her light up like a Christmas tree.

"Yup."

It's not a conventional clubhouse, but then we're not a conventional motorcycle club. We hang out at the bar, and there are club rooms out back for business. The courtyard behind the building has the brewery and the mechanic's shop.

"This isn't what I was expecting."

She crosses to the Harley on a pedestal in the corner. It's an ancient 1900s model from the original production line. It's my pride and joy but too old to ride, so I insisted we put it on display in the bar.

"You guys really love your bikes."

"We sure do."

Our conversation is interrupted by a booming voice.

"Vintage."

I look up at the sound of my road name.

A huge, bearded man is striding toward us. His eyes run over Danni, and jealousy flares up inside me. I put an arm around her waist, letting him know she's mine. Even though Lone Star is like a brother to me, the last thing I want is him thinking Danni is fair game.

"Lone Star." I introduce him to Danni, keeping my arm firmly around her waist.

"That your Caddy out back?"

Danni nods. "My pride and joy."

"It's a beauty."

Lone Star looks at her appreciatively. "The boys have replaced the valves, but the engine needs some TLC if you want to keep driving her around."

Danni squirms uncomfortably, and I wonder if it's the cost that's making her hesitate.

"Thanks. I'll just get the repair for now and do anything else when I get back."

The words bring the harsh reality of our situation into sharp focus. Tomorrow, Danni will drive out of here and back to her life. I thought I could handle this as a weekend thing, but the more time I've spent with her, the surer I am that I want more.

As I watch her talk to Lone Star about her Caddy and the bikes on display, I realize how she fits in here. It's like

Danni belongs in my life, like there was a place waiting here for her all along.

Lone Star leaves us alone, and I guide Danni across the road to the VIP seating area for the restaurant. It's on a platform that juts out over the valley and is the reason we get tourists from Hope making the drive over here to dine.

I choose a table by the window, smiling at Danni's reaction to the stunning view. The valley stretches below us, and from up here, it's like we're on the edge of the world.

The waitress comes over with two menus, and I order our drinks.

Danni leans over the menu. "Why did Lone Star call you Vintage?"

I smile, wondering if she was going to pick that up.

"It's my road name. We each have a road name, a nickname that the guys give you when you join."

"Lone Star is called Lone Star because he's a loner. Prefers his own company in the mountains when he's not working on a car. But his real name to anyone outside the club is Joseph."

"How did you get Vintage."

"Because I love vintage bikes."

She gives a short laugh. "The way I love vintage cars."

It's not lost on me how well suited we are. The thought makes me uncomfortable. I swore I'd never let a woman get close to me again. But I didn't know there was a woman like Danni out there.

The waitress comes over, and I'm happy for the distraction. We order the ribs to share and a plate of fries.

As we're waiting for our food to arrive, another one of my MC brothers strides into the bar. Word must have gotten around that I'm in here with woman, and now they've all come for a gander. I don't mind. I want to show Danni off. I want to show everyone that she's mine. Even if it's only for a weekend.

Travis, other wise knows as Hops, runs the Restaurant and Bar side of the business. He leans on the table. His gaze runs over Danni.

"Lone Star told me you had a woman in here. I had to see it for myself."

His gaze lingers on Danni too long, and an appreciative smile crosses his lip.

"Don't you have drinks to serve?" It comes out as a growl, and Hops gives me a startled look. It morphs into a knowing smirk when he sees my expression.

Quentin strides over to the table, breaking the tension.

"I've never seen Vintage bring a woman in here before. I had to check she wasn't a halucination."

Quentin's road name is Barrels on account of his stocky shape and the fact he runs the brewery. Him and Travis are old friends and when they both left the military they started the motorcycle club with Raiden, the club president.

I glower at the both of them.

"Sorry Danni. I didn't realize my MC brothers were going to be so immature."

Barrels ruffles my hair, and I swipe his arm out of the way.

"Then you don't know us at all, bro."

Thankfully, they don't stick around. We chat for a bit and then they head out back to get back to work.

Danni watches them go with a smile on her face. "They seem like a nice bunch of guys."

I guffaw. "Nice isn't a word I'd use to describe them."

But I'm smiling as I say it. I'll get the third degree at our next club meeting about Danni, but no matter how much we rib each other, I'd do anything for those guys. They're my brothers. I fought alongside some of them and ride beside all of them. I'd follow those men anywhere.

The food arrives, and Danni gives an excited squeak when she sees the enormous plate of ribs glistening with barbecue sauce. She tears a rib off and pulls the flesh apart with her teeth.

I love watching Danni eat. She eats with as much passion as she comes. Her inhibitions fall away around food as much as they do in the bedroom.

"So how does it feel?"

She swallows her mouthful, leaving a sticky glob of sauce at the side of her mouth. "How does what feel?"

"Doing what you want for the weekend."

She takes a sip of her soda and moans at the sugary hit.

"That's good. I haven't had a full fat Coke in ages." She ordered the full sugar version with a look of such delight that it made me laugh.

"It's feels wonderful, doing what I want for a change. This has been the best weekend I've ever had."

She looks down quickly, embarrassed by the admission. But her words make my heart skip a beat.

I reach across the table and take her hand.

"It's the best weekend I've ever had too."

She looks up at me shyly, and my heart melts. How am I going to give this woman up tomorrow? But it's selfish to think about me. Danni's had too much control in her life. She needs to make her own choices.

"But what happens after? What will Danni do when you go back home?"

"Good question." She sighs like the weight of the world's on her shoulders and looks out the window.

"I've got no job to go back to."

The frown lines are back on her face, and I hate myself for bringing it up. But maybe I can help Danni figure out what she wants to do with her life.

"I hated it. But at least it was a paycheck." She pushes a fry around her plate, smearing sauce everywhere. "Mom's already organized for my sister to get me an interview at her firm."

She says it as brightly as she can, but I can tell she's not happy about it.

"Is that what you want to do?"

"Mel works for the biggest finance company in the city. It would be a step up."

"But is it what *you* want to do?"

Danni sighs again and shrugs her shoulders. "I don't know. It's good money, good prospects. Mom's only looking out for me. She wants me to be successful."

She keeps looking down at her plate, and I get the pressure she's under. But I can't imagine a girl like Danni fitting in at a finance company.

"If your weekend of yes continued when you got back home, if you could ask for any job, any career, and it would be yours, what would you do?"

"I'd start my own business."

There's no hesitation in her answer. Danni's thought about this before.

"Doing what?"

She drops her gaze again. "It's a stupid idea."

"Try me."

"I mean, it's a great idea, but I went to business school, it's not the kind of life-changing idea that will make me a millionaire."

"Danni, would you rather be a millionaire, or would you rather be happy?"

She tilts her head, looking at me. She's smart, and I'm sure that whatever she turns her hand to will be successful.

"When you put it like that…"

"So, tell me about this idea."

"Well, I love vintage fifties stuff. There are a lot of collectors out there, and there are a lot of artists doing things that have a fifties vibe. I had this idea to bring them together."

"A studio?"

"Exactly." Her eyes light up, and she gets animated as she talks. "An exhibition space as well as an online shop. I also do some artwork myself."

She says the last bit shyly.

My admiration for her grows. This woman is full of surprises.

"What kind of art?"

"I draw. Sketches mostly. I love the fifties aesthetic."

She pulls out her phone and flips to a photo. It's a drawing of a woman's face. Her hair is up in a fifties do, and her eyes are sad. She looks wistfully to the left of the frame. It's sexy and smart and it's bold.

"You drew this?"

She nods, biting her lower lip. "I've never shown anyone before."

"Princess, this is amazing."

Her frown turns into a smile. "You really think so?"

"Absolutely. You could sell these for sure. If you want to. Hell, I'll buy this first one for the cabin."

She laughs as if I'm joking. But I'm not. The woman's got talent and an idea that would fit in around here. My brain goes into overdrive at the possibilities.

"You could find a studio…" I'm about to add here, in the mountains. But I'm interrupted by Danni's phone ringing. Her face falls when she looks at the number.

"Everything all right?"

"It's Mom." She sighs heavily. "I could never get my studio idea going. Mom wouldn't approve."

She looks at her phone but doesn't answer it. I don't know what hold her mom has on her, but it's time to let it go.

My hand closes over hers. It's time someone gave her permission to be herself.

"Your mom's holding you back, Danni. You're a talented, smart woman with a business degree. If you want to start a vintage art studio, you can do it. I believe in you."

She looks at the phone ringing in her hand.

Then, suddenly, she lifts it up and flings it out the window. The phone sails over the cliff's edge and falls into the canopy of trees below.

Her stunned expression matches my own. We stare at each other. Then Danni bursts out laughing. It's a wonderful sound, the sound of someone who's truly free.

"You're right, Colter. I'm done with trying to please my mom. It's time I pleased myself."

My heart lifts with pride. She's going after what she wants. I just hope I'm included on that list.

9
DANNI

I wake the next morning with a mixture of excitement and loss. Excited because I finally know what I want to do with my life, and I won't let Mom stop me. And loss because this is the last day I'll be waking up in Colter's arms.

We fooled around last night like we've been doing ever since the rocky pool. He did wicked things with his tongue. But I've not felt him inside me yet. I want to go all the way with him, but he hasn't suggested it, and it's too embarrassing to ask. What if he says no? There must be a reason he's been holding back. He told me he doesn't do relationships, and maybe that's it.

Over breakfast, Colter gets the call that my car is ready.

Everything about packing my bag feels heavy. I try to make it last, knowing these will be the last few moments

I spend with Colter. But too soon I'm packed, and there's no excuse to stay any longer.

I give Daisy a final pat goodbye and she looks at me dolefully, reflecting exactly how I feel.

"You get the bike all to yourself again, girl." But the big dog only whines and rests her head on her paws.

I slide onto the back of Colter's bike, trying not to let him see the emotions churning inside me. He seems surprisingly calm about all of this. And it just illustrates how inexperienced I am with men. He told me it was just for the weekend, but my big, stupid heart went and fell for him anyway.

Last night while we watched a movie he was on his phone a lot, and he went out to take a call. I guess this weekend is ending for him too, and he's moving on to life without me.

The ride to the clubhouse seems too short, and soon we're pulling into the courtyard behind the bar. The mechanic's shop is directly behind the bar, but Colter crosses the courtyard, passes the brewery, and rides right over to one of the other buildings in the compound.

"I want to show you something."

He seems excited, and that hurts. I'm too despondent to be interested in anything, and it's clear he's not sad at all about me leaving. Without paying much attention, I get off the bike and follow him to a building that's on the edge of the courtyard.

Colter slides the door open. It's one of those old-fashioned sliding wooden doors with peeling green paint.

Inside is nothing but a wooden workbench and some old paint cans. The single window is boarded up, and dust motes dance in a slit of light that peeks through the gaps.

"What do you think?"

I squint at Colter, not sure what he means. It just looks like a storage shed to me.

"About what?"

"A lick of paint and a good cleaning. You could put glass back in the windows for more light."

I still don't know what he's talking about, but based on the smile on his face, he seems pretty pleased with himself. Which just adds to my irritation. I'm devastated to be leaving, and he's showing me a creaky old workshop.

"Can I just get my car?"

I turn my back to the shed. I just want to get out of here now to get in my car and drive away before I break down.

Colter takes me by the shoulders and spins me around. With one arm around my shoulders, he gestures with the other arm.

"Your studio could be at the back, once the window's fixed. And the front part could be a gallery and shop."

Studio… shop… The words break through my foggy brain. Does he mean…?

"You think this could be my studio?"

My chest flutters, and hope fills my heart. Colter nods as the realization hits me.

"You found me a studio? Here?" Does that mean he wants me to stay?

He's grinning like the cat that got the cream, and there's something else in his expression. Hope.

"Do you like it?"

I step into the shed and really look at it for the first time.

When the window's fixed, it will get the morning sun. Perfect for sketching. The space is long and narrow, and I can imagine rows of artwork and display cases.

The location is perfect. This side of the courtyard stretches to the left of the bar. The gallery would be seen from the road, and anyone stopping in at the bar or brewery could stop by for a look.

Then there are the tourists that come to the mountains. If I dropped brochures in all the tourist venues, it could be a destination shop.

A funny sensation pools in my stomach and makes my body tingle with the possibilities.

"Colter, it's perfect. But..." I can't finish what I want to say, because I'm afraid of his answer.

His expression turns serious, and he takes a step toward me. "But what, Danni? Tell me this isn't what you want, that you don't want to stay?"

I'm taken off balance. Colter told me he doesn't do relationships, that this was just for the weekend. Does he really want me to stick around?

"But how about you? What do you want?"

His hand brushes my cheek. "Danni, I want you. Since

the moment I saw you leaning on a 1956 Caddy, I wanted you. I tried to tell myself it could just be for the weekend, but I was wrong."

"I thought you didn't do relationships?"

"Neither did I. I was hurt once. When I went on my first tour, I came back and my girlfriend was with someone else. I swore I'd never get close to a woman again. But over the years, it's become a habit rather than a conviction. I thought I was okay on my own until I met you.

"I want you, Danni, and not just for the weekend. I want you for life."

My breath hitches. It's everything I hoped he'd say to me.

"If you want it, there's a life here for you, Danni. I arranged it with the guys last night. No one uses this building anymore. You can have it on lease, and I've paid for the first six months. Even if you don't want me, you can take the building. But you've got to make sure this is what *you* want. You have to tell me what you want."

I think about Mom and the dozens of messages she'll be leaving on my defunct phone. I think of the years I've spent trying to please her and how miserable I've been. I think about the last few days on the mountain, of Colter and the way I feel when I'm with him. No one makes me feel like he does. I've never felt freer or more myself. So what do I, Danni Malone really want?

There's only one thing I want, and he's staring at me with a hopeful look in his eyes.

"I want you, Colter. I want this. All of it. I want to stay with you on the mountain. It's what I want for myself."

His lips press against mine, and a sigh escapes me. His kiss feels so right. Our bodies press against each other, and his hardness pushes into me.

With his foot, Colter kicks back and pushes the door. It slides closed, shutting out the light.

"What are you doing?"

"Now that I know you truly want me, I'm claiming you."

A delicious shiver goes through me, and my panties dampen. I like the sound of that.

10
COLTER

Danni wants me. She's going to stay, and she's all mine. The thought makes my dick twitch, ready to claim her. I grind my hips into her, and she rolls against me so I sink into her curves.

"Danni..."

My lips brush against her neck and I inhale her scent, getting high on the feeling of having her in my arms and knowing she's all mine. I walk her backwards until she bumps up against the wooden bench. Then I lift her hips and slide her onto the bench. There's a sliver of light from the boarded up window throwing her features into dark shadow. I've never seen her look more beautiful, knowing she's mine. Mine to keep.

My hands slide over her thighs, and I hitch up the billowy skirt she's wearing. Her skin is pale in the darkness and I run my fingertips over her thighs, right up to the wet patch between her legs.

"You're wet already, Princess."

The fact that she's already wet for me turns me on so much.

"I'm wet for you." Her voice comes out breathy as I slide my finger under her panties and slip between her folds.

"Good girl."

Her eyes widen at the praise and she sticks her chest out, giving me an eyeful of her gorgeous breasts. She wants to please me, and I love that.

Taking my time, I slide my finger out of her pussy and bring it to my lips. Her sweet taste fills my senses as I suck her juices off my finger. So sweet and all mine.

She's wearing a 1950s style knee length skirt, and I bunch it up so I can pull her panties down. They drop to the floor and I part her thighs, keeping her skirt around her hips so I can see her pussy. It's magnificent and glistening in the dim light. My cock jerks at the sight, and I can't get my pants off fast enough.

Her hand fumbles at my belt until my cock pops out. Then I step between her thighs and line myself up with her entrance. The edge of her skirt slips down so I can't see her pussy anymore. I'm encased in polka-dot fabric with the heat of her arousal surrounding my cock and drawing it in. It's dirty and erotic, and I restrain myself from pumping straight into her.

I should take Danni home and lie her down on a bed and make love to her slowly. But my instinct is too raw. I have to have her now. And there's something sexy about her keeping her clothes on while I fuck her. My cock disappears under her skirts, and heat shoots up me as I graze her pussy.

She shudders and leans back on the bench as I run my cock over her sticky folds.

"You like that?"

She nods slowly, her eyes hooded.

"I need to hear you say it."

Danni bites her lower lip and looks at me coyly. That innocent look sends a new bolt of sensation up my cock and I jerk forward, my tip sinking into her.

Her eyes widen at the sudden intrusion, and her mouth pops open.

"I like it, Colter," she gasps.

I love hearing my name on her lips, and I want to hear her scream it. She's so damn sexy I can't hold back anymore.

"You ready for this, Princess?"

"Yes."

She's breathless as I push further into her tight opening. Danni squeezes her eyes shut.

"Eyes on me, Danni." I pause with my cock tip inside her. She opens her eyes, and they lock on mine. She's panting hard as I inch into her. She's so fucking tight my dick feels like it's in a vice. It's so good and so crushing all at once. I give her another inch, and her eyes go wider.

My cock pushes up against her virgin barrier and I pause, feeling the weight of the moment. There's no going back from here. As we gaze into each other's eyes, my heart opens. I don't want to go back. I want this woman by my side, and I want her pussy clamped around me every day for the rest of my life.

"I love you, Danni."

Her eyes go soft and she blinks quickly, fighting back tears. "I love you too, Colter."

"You're my good girl."

She whimpers and I use the moment to thrust hard, bursting through her hymen and sinking deep into her virgin pussy.

Danni gasps, but her eyes remain open. I see every emotion as it claims her, the fear, the pain, and the satisfaction as her pussy adjusts to my cock.

As she relaxes, I let my needs surface, sliding out of her just to feel her pussy tug on my cock. With gentle motions, I pump into her, grabbing her ass and pulling her up and down my dick.

Her eyebrows knit together in wonder, and it's the sexiest thing I've ever seen.

"It's… Colter… It feels so good."

"It's meant to, Princess."

She smiles, and it turns into a moan as I thrust deep. My fingers hook her hips and I pull her down my shaft, until I'm coated in her pussy juices and virgin blood.

Her moans turn to little cries, and I know she's close to release. I pull her toward me and she rocks her hips, getting the friction she needs. She writhes against me and I feel her pressure build, making my own cock lengthen.

"Come like a good girl, Danni, like my good little wife."

Her eyes go wide at the word, and at that moment she falls apart. Her pussy convulses around me, and the sensation makes my dick explode.

I let myself go, shooting hot cum deep inside of her, hoping that my seed will find her womb and start growing our child.

Afterwards I pull her close, and she clings on to me sleepily.

"Did you mean what you said?"

She worries her bottom lip, which make me smile.

"About being my wife?"

She nods shyly.

"Princess, I'm gonna put a ring on your finger and a baby in your belly just as soon as I can. You're mine forever."

She smiles happily and leans her head against my chest. A warm contentment washes over me.

I thought my life was good, just me, the club, my bikes, and my dog. I didn't know I was missing Danni until she turned up on the side of my mountain. Life is good, but with Danni by my side, it's going to be a wild ride.

EPILOGUE

DANNI

Four years later…

"I'm so glad we stopped by," gushes the woman in the pea-green sun hat. "We only stopped in for lunch and saw your place next to the restaurant…"

It's a familiar story and how I attract most of my customers. Colter was right all those years ago. This is the perfect spot for a boutique studio.

I wrap the framed print in tissue paper for the woman as she gushes about her new purchase. It makes me happy serving customers like this lady who'll get a lot of joy from her print.

"I'll tell the other girls you're here. We're staying at the Emerald Heart Lodge, and I saw the brochure."

There's a tug on my skirt and I glance down at the anxious face of Bettie, my two-and-a-half year old.

"Hungry."

She doesn't mince words in telling me what she wants. The customer's face goes soft at the sight of my little girl as I scoop her into my arms.

"Oh, what a sweetheart."

Bettie beams at the lady and reaches for her hat. I intercept her chubby hand before she can pull it off the lady's head.

The woman takes the parcel and heads outside, another satisfied customer.

"Hungry," Bettie says again.

"Should we go see Daddy for lunch?"

She nods, making her dark curls jump up and down.

At that moment, one of the MC prospects steps into the studio. Davis is about the same age as me, but his serious expression makes him seem older. He got an honorable discharge from the military and found his way to Wild Heart Mountain and the Wild Heart MC.

"Perfect timing."

One of the guys always comes over to watch the shop while I go for lunch. When I married Colter, I became part of the family. The club helps each other out with big things, like building a brother a new cabin, and small things, like watching the shop while I go for lunch. I've got a whole family here on the mountain.

I head out of the sliding door, painted a fresh ocean blue, and into the sunlight. The scent of hops from the brewery hits my nostrils, but I'm used to it now. The afternoon tour is just beginning, and I'm sure to pick up some business afterwards when the tourists wander around the small group of boutique shops that has sprung up in the courtyard.

Bettie clasps my hand as she toddles across to the workshop. It's on the other side of the brewery, tucked in the corner.

Colter looks up from the bike he's working on and gives a wide grin when he sees us. He wipes his hand on a rag and straightens up from his bike. It's his own bike he's working on today. His Harley Fat Bob. The one we take out most often for everyday riding.

A small, hard, plastic seat rests at the back of the bike seat.

"What's this?"

Colter runs a hand over the seat, and I notice the straps coming off it.

"A child seat. This one's getting old enough now to ride pillion."

I knew this day was coming. Colter's been wanting to get Bettie on a bike since the day she was born. I had to convince him to wait until she could at least keep her own head up.

He picks Bettie up, and she gives a squeal as he sits her on the seat.

"How does that feel, little one?"

She makes motorbike noises, her chubby cheeks blowing out raspberries.

Drawn to the noise, Daisy jumps up on the bike in front of her.

"You're gonna have to give up your seat, old girl." I run a hand over the aging dog's head.

"No, she won't."

Colter gestures to a sidecar next to the bike.

"You're going to put Daisy in the sidecar?"

He grins. "I've turned this into the family bike."

I love that my husband is always thinking about us. How he adapted his life to fit me in. Well, he's going to have to adapt again, once I tell him the news that I confirmed this morning.

I bite my lower lip, not sure how he'll take it.

His gaze dips to my lip. "Oh no, what is it?"

He knows me so well. I slide my arm around him and lean back to see his reaction to my news.

"You're gonna have to make room for one more."

He looks confused for a moment until realization dawns.

"You're pregnant?"

I nod, the smile spreading across my face. Colter gives a whoop so loud that Daisy barks, which sets Bettie off crying.

We laugh as he scoops Bettie up and slides his other arm around me.

"You've just made me the happiest man on the mountain."

It's been a wild ride the last four years. It wasn't easy telling Mom I was moving here. She cried and begged for me to come back, telling me all the ways it was going to go wrong for me.

I had to set boundaries for her, and we didn't speak for six months. But when I had Bettie, I reached out to her and she softened. She accepted Colter over time and begrudgingly agreed that my business is a success.

We have an easier relationship now, and she comes and stays every few months.

It was the best thing I ever did coming here and meeting Colter. He taught me to go after what I want and then gave me the freedom to get it.

But really the only thing I want is him and our family.

Daisy jumps off the bike and pushes between us, never wanting to be left out.

I rub her big head, and she rests it against my belly. I'm sure she already knows what's growing inside. Dogs have a sense about those things.

Colter plants a kiss on my lips, and a familiar spark jumps between us.

"I'm so happy, Princess." His eyes crinkle, and I know he's telling the truth. We both got our happy ending. We both got what we want.

* * *

WILD HOPE

WILD HOPE

Why is forbidden love the sweetest?

When Kendra turns up at the Wild Riders MC compound looking for a job, I'm in agony.

I've been in love with my best friend's little sister since she waved us off for Iraq. I served with her brother. He's my best friend, my MC brother, and my business partner.

If I act on my feelings for his little sister, I'll not only dishonor my best friend, I'll be banished from the club.

But when a customer gets handsy with Kendra, my protective instincts kick in. I'll fight anyone and everyone to be with Kendra, whatever the price.

Wild Hope is a big brother's best friend, forbidden love, age gap romance featuring an ex-military mountain man and the curvy, innocent woman who claims his heart.

1
TRAVIS

The coffee burns my throat on the way down, and the bitterness sets my taste buds on edge.

I swallow the bitter brew and slide the cup back to Maggie.

"More cream."

"Sorry," she mumbles.

I try not to let her see me sigh. Maggie was only supposed to help out in the kitchen, but when a waitress quit last week, I convinced her to help out in the restaurant for a few shifts. The poor girl's as shy as a door mouse and as jumpy as one too.

"Don't worry about it." I give her a reassuring smile while making a mental note that we need to expedite finding new staff. "I'll cover the rest of the shift."

There're only two tables left, and we're not likely to get many drop-ins on a Monday afternoon.

Maggie gives me a grateful look and scurries out the back. She's a competent cook, but the woman doesn't know how to make coffee to save herself.

I skate around the back of the bar and tip out the sorry excuse for a brew. There's a sealed bag of Brazil's strongest coffee beans, and when I open it a rich aroma fills my nostrils. I breathe in deep and tip a bunch of beans into the grinder.

Wild Taste Bar and Restaurant is known for its craft beer, due to the brewery out back, but we also serve the best coffee on this side of the mountain.

With the beans freshly ground, I fill the porter filter and make myself the perfect cup.

A few minutes later, I'm back on my black metal barstool taking the first sip.

"Mmmm," I say to no one in particular. "That's good coffee."

While I wait for the caffeine to hit my bloodstream, I glance over the bar. Bike memorabilia adorns the walls with a vintage Harley taking pride of place. There're photos of the motorcycle club riding out for a charity event in our full Wild Riders MC leather jackets, and then the members dressed in their military uniforms for a Veterans Day parade.

The restaurant's unusual in that it's split in two. The bar opens up to a dining area, and there's a VIP section over the road perched on the edge of the cliff face. The views from that side are stunning, looking over the valley below.

We've had to keep it closed the last few weeks due to staff shortages. It's hard to keep the service running on both sides when you're a waitress down.

I've been helping where I can, but on top of my regular workload, I'm exhausted.

As a founding member of the Wild Riders MC and manager of the Wild Taste Bar and Restaurant, there's a lot to do. The MC club owns the businesses, but Quentin and I run the place.

We've opened the brewery up for tours, and it's not going as smoothly as I'd like. The marketing has been too effective. Every tourist on both sides of the mountain wants a brewery tour, and we're booked up solid for the next several weeks. We're extending the tour times and hours, but so far there's no one to run them.

It's hard to get staff to stick around in the ass end of nowhere.

What attracted a bunch of ex-military bikers to a place is not the same as what most people want. After the military, I came here with my best friend Quentin and bike mad Raiden. It was the perfect spot to regroup, recover, and get our asses going on the next stage of life.

It was Raiden's idea to start the Wild Riders MC club, and he became president. Our compound comprises the group of businesses that have sprung up on the side of the mountain: the restaurant, the brewery, and the bike repair shop out back. We've got clubrooms at the back of the restaurant and rooms upstairs for whoever needs them.

The closest town, Wild, is a twenty minute ride away. And that's how we like it. Quiet, remote, and isolated. Perfect for a bunch of damaged soldiers.

But it turns out not everyone wants to live in the mountains. There are plenty of tourists to keep the bills paid, but finding staff who want to live in the middle of nowhere is a problem.

It's rare to get a quiet moment, and I sip my coffee and let my mind wander. As it so often does, I think about how good I have it up here: a thriving business, a cabin in the woods, my MC club with brothers who'd do anything for me. Yet, in still moments like these, there's a restlessness in my soul, a feeling like I'm missing something, like I got it all wrong.

I survey my restaurant. The table of tourists pouring over brochures, the couple finishing their lunch in the corner, the bikes parked out front, the noises from the kitchen as Chef preps for the evening trade, and the smell of hops from the brewery which permeates my clothes and is how I got my road name: Hops.

I should be happy, I should be content, yet there's something missing.

Like I've done so many times in moments like these, I pull out my wallet and slide the dog-eared photo out of the card holder. Me and Quentin stand upright in military uniforms. Between us is a woman with blonde hair falling over her shoulders. She's wearing shorts that show off thick creamy thighs and one leg is bent, her knee bending in towards the other, her heel in the air. Her smile is wide and lights up her sparkling eyes, which are the same deep green as the forest canopy.

I pulled this photo out so many times in Iraq that the paper is worn thin and there are spiderweb lines where it's creased around the edges. But Kendra's smile is as bright as it was the day the photo was taken six years ago.

Kendra was only eighteen when that photo was taken. Unaware of how her short shorts and throaty laugh made my entire body stir with desire. I suppressed it. She was an innocent girl and I was a man of twenty-nine, who had seen too much and was jaded by life. Besides, Kendra's my best friend's little sister. Off limits.

My parents moved to Australia once I left for the military, so Quentin invited me to spend Thanksgiving leave with his family.

Mrs. Harrison cooked a Thanksgiving feast, and we played board games. I spent the entire two weeks trying to keep my eyes off Kendra as she moved around the house, singing pop songs and dancing every chance she got.

That was before the accident that claimed her parents. Before her and Quentin's world fell into darkness.

Quentin left the army after his parents passed, and I soon followed. I visited my parents in Cairns, sweating like I was back in the desert. Then I followed Quentin to the cooler mountain.

By then Kendra was on the road, spending her inheritance and trying to outrun her grief.

Quentin used some of his inheritance for a down payment on the brewery, Raiden chipped in, and I used my military savings to stump up the other third, and the Wild Riders MC was born.

Life has been busy, life has been good, but I find myself pulling out the picture and studying Kendra's face more often than I like to admit.

"You haven't changed a bit."

I glance up at the throaty voice, and there she is. In the flesh. Kendra Harrison. All five foot two of her, blonde hair streaked with bright pink cascading over her shoulders, wearing knee-high leather boots and a skirt as short as the shorts in the photo.

My jaw hits the floor, and I want to grab my coat and cover her legs. No one sees those thighs but me.

Her smile is as broad as in the picture, but it doesn't quite reach her eyes. The cheeks are fuller, and she's lost the little girl look. Her figure has filled out; she's a woman now, with womanly curves a man could get lost in.

"Kendra." It's the dumbest thing to say, but I can't believe she's really here. "What are you doing here?"

She raises an eyebrow at me. "Good to see you too, Travis. Or should I call you Hops now?"

She's referring to my road name, which means she must have been in touch with Quentin. Son of a bitch never told me.

"Call me Travis." Damn, that sounds awkward. Like I've just met her, not like I spent Thanksgiving at her house and the last six years thinking about her.

Her eyes sparkle like she's enjoying my discomfort. "It's good to see you, Travis."

She dumps the duffle bag she's holding and strides over to where I'm sitting, the heels of her leather boots clacking against the wooden floor and turning the heads of my customers.

I slide off the bar stool, still stunned by her presence when she wraps her arms around me.

Her hair smells like peppermint, and her perfume is musky. Her body is soft, and her feminine curves pressed against me cause my blood to heat. I hug her back, just as she pulls away.

Her arms loosen, and she kisses me on the cheek. Like a brother. She kisses me like a brother.

"There she is."

Quentin's deep voice rumbles across the bar, and I drop my arms guiltily as if he can see into my mind.

"Quentin." She squeals and runs at her brother. He sweeps her into his arms and twirls her around, making Kendra giggle. A jealous twinge rumbles through my heart. I want to make Kendra giggle like that.

"How did you get here?" Quentin asks. "I wasn't expecting you until tomorrow."

She holds her thumb out and Quentin frowns.

"You hitched?" We both say it at the same time.

Kendra rolls her eyes. "Geez, it's like having two overprotective big brothers. Yeah, I hitched from the closest town. Got a lift from a pregnant lady in a Caddy."

"Danni," I say, feeling relieved. Danni just married Vintage. Colter is his real name, but he goes by Vintage on account of his love for old bikes. It's not surprising he hooked up with a woman who drives an old Cadillac.

"Do you all know each other around here?"

"You're lucky Danni picked you up, but I don't want you hitching again." Quentin uses his stern big brother voice, but Kendra shakes her head at him.

"I don't think you can stop me, big brother."

Quentin turns a shade of purple, and I must look the same. There's no way I'm letting Kendra hitch a lift ever again. But before he can say anything else, Kendra puts her hand on his shoulder.

"Relax. I'm not going anywhere for a while anyway."

My heart skips a beat at her words. "You sticking around?"

"Didn't my brother tell you?" I look to Quentin, but he's got his eyes on his sister. He didn't tell me she was coming, and it makes me wonder if he knows how I feel about her. "He said you needed help, and here I am."

The thought of Kendra working here, working alongside me where I can see her every day, makes my stomach flip.

At that moment one of the prospects walks past, and Quentin picks up Kendra's bag and hands it to him.

"Show Kendra to her room. She's taking the blue

room upstairs until I can find her a place to stay. First shift's tonight. If you're up for it."

"Sure thing, big bro. Anything to help." She follows the prospect out of the room and I stare after her, trying to process what's going on.

Kendra is here, she's staying upstairs, and she'll be working in my restaurant for the foreseeable future. I'll get to spend every day with her, to watch her move, to talk and laugh with her.

"Can I count on you?"

I don't realize Quentin's been talking to me until he snaps his fingers. "Hey, Hops, where did you go?"

To an alternate universe where I wake up every morning next to your sister. But I don't say that.

"Sorry bro, just a lot on my plate."

"I'm on this work trip later in the week."

Quentin and the Prez are going on a road trip to visit some of our distributors and try to drum up more business. I'm staying behind this time to keep things running.

"I want you to keep an eye on Kendra for me. Help her settle in and make sure none of the guys get any ideas. I love my brothers, but if anyone lays a finger on my sister, they're out of the club."

He cracks his knuckles, and his face tells me he's serious.

"She's been through enough shit, and the last thing she needs is any grease monkey trying anything with her. I'll break the nose of any man who so much as asks her the time."

He slaps me on the back. "Can I count on you to keep an eye on her while I'm gone?"

I swallow hard, swallowing down the brief fantasy of anything I might have imagined for me and Kendra. Quentin's made it clear; she's off limits.

"Sure," I say, trying to smile. "You can count on me."

2
KENDRA

"Drinks for table nine."

The bartender moves two wine glasses out of the way to fit the last beer on the tray. I have to use two hands to pick it up and carry it over to the rowdy table in the corner. I take at least a minute to weave between the busy tables, stopping as a woman pushes her seat back right in front of me, nearly spilling the entire tray of drinks.

"Sorry, I didn't see you."

"No problem." I'm the queen of patience, having waitressed across the country for the last six years. It's all about smiling and waiting and keeping it together no matter what happens.

I set the drinks down at the table and collect the empty glasses.

Both the evening shifts I've worked have been like

this. I'm happy for my brother that the place is so busy. Business is good for him and the club.

I'm on my way back to the bar with the tray of glasses when Travis saunters in. My feet stumble, and water sloshes over the side of one glass. I catch myself before the entire tray goes down.

Damn, that man can still make me lose my balance.

I thought six years might have dulled my feelings, but when I saw him sitting at the bar this afternoon, his biker jacket on, a layer of messy stubble over his strong jaw, and silver flecked through his hair, my heartbeat went up several notches and it hasn't come back down. Now my palms are sweaty, and I'm having trouble concentrating on my tables.

I thought my girly crush on my brother's best friend might have dulled, but nope. It's turned from a girly crush to a womanly longing. One look at Travis's broad shoulders and tight white t-shirt and there's damp heat between my legs and my nipples are tingling.

Too bad he's not interested.

My hair falls across my face, and I curse myself for the pink streaks I've had for the last few years. I thought it looked edgy and cool, but to a man like Travis it probably shows how young I still am. His hair is peppered with silver, and there are crinkles at the sides of his eyes. He's the kind of man that needs a woman, not a too-chunky girl playing dress up.

"Excuse me. Can I get some ketchup?"

The woman's voice snaps me out of my thoughts, and

I turn to her. "Sure." I give her my best smile. "I'll bring it right over."

I deposit the glasses at the bar and grab a bottle of ketchup to take back to the lady.

"Food's up for table eleven," the slight girl in the kitchen calls.

I give the lady her ketchup and head over to the serving hatch. As I walk past the bar, the skin on the back of my neck prickles. Glancing up, I catch Travis watching me. His dark eyes dart up from my butt, and he looks away.

Did I just catch him checking me out?

All kinds of heat courses through my body, and I wipe my palms on my apron as I get to the serving hatch.

"Someone can't take their eyes off you." Maggie waggles her eyebrows, and I glance back to see Travis staring at me again.

"He's been watching you all night," Maggie whispers. "Again."

Her mousy brown hair is pinned up under a chef's hat, showing off her round face dusted in freckles. I met Maggie when I arrived yesterday and liked her immediately. She's supposed to be a cook but has been helping anyway she can in the kitchen. She's quiet but observant and will be one hell of a chef one day.

I don't know where my brother found her, but she's so petite she looks like a kid working in the kitchen.

"I've known Travis for years," I say, trying to brush it off. "He's just being friendly."

"Uh-huh," she says with a knowing smile.

The plates are slippery in my sweaty palms, and my feet seem to have trouble walking. I wish Travis would disappear into the back office so I could get on with waitressing without feeling like my knees are about to give way.

I deliver the food to table eleven. There are a bunch of empty glasses and I clear them off the table, holding the tray over my head and maneuvering through the crowded restaurant to get back to the bar.

Arlo, the bartender, is preparing a sampling board for table thirteen. They're a bunch of hipsters who must be staying at the ski lodge judging by the way they're dressed. They're the only ones here whose flannel shirts look freshly pressed and whose beards are neatly trimmed.

I shake my head to myself, marveling at what a good thing my brother has going on here. The brewery provides decent beer for the locals and craft beer for visiting hipsters just like these.

I scoot around the side of the bar with my tray of glasses, thinking I'll put them in the dishwasher since Arlo is busy.

I don't notice Travis until I get around behind the bar. He's crouched down restocking the fridge. He stands up abruptly, and I run straight into the solid muscles of his chest. My feet stumble, my breath leaves my chest, and this time there's no saving the glasses.

The tray goes down. Glass shatters everywhere. The

smashing sound silences the restaurant, and all heads turn to me.

There's a moment of utter silence. Then someone claps and the restaurant cheers, and everyone goes back to eating.

"I'm so sorry."

My cheeks heat with embarrassment. Of all the people to run into, it had to be Travis. I drop to the floor at the same time as he does, almost bumping heads. I pick up shards of glass, trying to ignore the fact that I'm so close to him I can smell his scent of hops and some musky male body wash.

"It's okay. I'll take it out of your pay."

I glance up at him, and his lips twitch. "I'm kidding. It happens all the time."

Now he's being nice. I've been waitressing for the last six years, and not once have I dropped an entire tray of glasses or seen anyone drop an entire tray of glasses. Travis must think I'm an incompetent klutz.

"I don't know what happened." I pile broken glass onto the tray while embarrassment claws at my skin. "I didn't expect you to be hiding behind the bar."

He chuckles, and it's a deep throaty rumble that I feel in my bones.

"I was stocking the fridge. I didn't mean to startle you."

He startled me the moment I walked in the door. I came back to help my brother and to see if my feelings for Travis had changed. That's a big nope.

Travis's hand shoots out and clasps me around the wrist. Heat from his touch skitters through my body, and my breath hitches.

"You've cut yourself."

I glance down at my hand, and there's a thin trickle of blood oozing from my index finger.

"Damn."

Travis lets go of my wrist, and I slip my finger between my lips. A metallic taste hits my tongue as I suck hard to stem the blood flow.

Travis makes a strangled noise, and I glance up at him. He's staring at my mouth as I suck the finger between my lips.

His pupils dilate, and a low growl rumbles from his chest that I feel all the way to my core. My skin heats with embarrassment as I realize what this must look like, even as heat floods my panties at the hungry way he's looking at me.

Travis stands up quickly, and the moment passes.

"Get a bandage on that. I'll get this cleaned up."

He saunters out of the bar area without looking back.

I watch him go with a new lightness in my chest. Travis *is* attracted to me, I'm sure of it. If only I can get him to see me as something other than Quentin's little sister.

3
TRAVIS

My palms are sweating, my blood is thundering in my ears, and my dick's as hard as the trunk of a pine tree in the forest.

It's bad enough that Kendra's been wiggling her curvy ass all night, her hips swaying as she weaves through the restaurant. I haven't been able to keep my eyes off her body. Then she goes and crashes right into me, her tits bouncing off my chest and the scent of flowers and perspiration trailing after her. But when she slipped her finger between her plump lips and sucked on it, I almost lost control.

An image of her full lips wrapped around my cock jumped into my head and I had to get out of there before I did something stupid, like throw her over the bar and claim her in front of the entire restaurant.

Because she's not mine to claim. She's Quentin's little sister, and there's no way she'll ever be mine. Not that she'd want an old man like me anyway. Kendra's a free spirit. She's been on the road ever since her parents died, moving from town to town doing work here and there.

Quentin's been worried sick about her, and so have I. Now that she's here, he'll do anything to make her stay. Which means I can't hit on her, even if I thought she wanted me. I can't fuck this up and have her leaving town. She's safe here, even if she can't be mine.

"Busy night out there?"

I jump at the sound of Quentin's voice, and he chuckles.

"What you so jumpy for?"

Because I'm this close to throwing your little sister over my shoulder and carrying her to my cabin.

I run my hand through my hair and try to hide what I'm really thinking.

"No reason, bro. Just a busy night."

He leans on the doorframe of the office, casting his face into shadow.

"You sure you'll be all right on your own with me and the Prez gone?"

Geez, I must be jumpy if he needs to ask that. "Yeah, I've got it under control. Especially with Kendra here and Arlo helping at the bar. The restaurant is almost fully staffed."

"About Kendra…"

He takes a step into the office, and I tense. Has he read my thoughts, or am I just that obvious?

"Like I said the other day, I need you to watch her while I'm away."

My shoulders relax. He doesn't know the thoughts I've been having about her. He doesn't know that I'm the one who needs watching.

"I'll look out for her."

"Now that she's here, I want her to stay. I want her close so I can keep an eye on her."

The thought of Kendra living on the mountain, where I could see her every day, makes my heart sing. I won't have to pull out the photo. The real thing will be here.

"Make sure none of the guys try anything."

His voice goes serious, and he cracks his knuckles. "I don't want some asshole treating her bad and scaring her off."

The thought of another man with his hands on Kendra makes my fists clench.

"I'll make sure."

"Good. I'll kill any fucker who messes with her."

I nod. And he claps me on the shoulder, a grin returning to his face.

"Thanks, man. See you when we get back."

Quentin leaves the office, and I lean on the side of the desk. He wants me to watch his little sister, but he doesn't realize I'm the one he should be worried about.

4
KENDRA

It's a few nights later, and only two tables remain in the restaurant.

One is a couple in the corner holding hands over the table. I'm trying not to feel envious of their easy laughter and the way they've spent the night talking and touching.

"That's Kobe and Hailey."

Arlo catches me watching them and leans against the bar next to me. There's a note of envy in his voice too. I guess I'm not the only one wishing I had a love like that.

"I served with Kobe. He's a good guy. They live on the other side of the mountain, near Hope. But we don't hold that against them."

The only other table is a group of hipsters that were on the brewery tour this afternoon. They've spent the entire evening since in the bar. What started as a sampling of craft beer led to downing pints like water and breaking into song.

"I've given them their last orders," Arlo tells me. "A taxi's on its way to take them back to the lodge."

"There's a taxi service around here?"

Arlo grins. "We've got a guy who comes up from Wild. He's not a registered taxi. Just uses his car occasionally to collect drunks like these."

I feel a tingle down my spine and look up to find Travis watching me. He's perched on a stool at the end of the bar with his laptop in front of him. There's a scowl on his face and Arlo must see it, because he pushes off the bar and away from me.

"Better get back to work," he mumbles.

Travis has been here all night, helping when needed but mostly tapping away on his keyboard while nursing a beer.

I've felt his eyes on me throughout the night, and every time I look up, I've caught him looking at me. He doesn't even bother to look away. He just keeps those intense eyes on me, his gaze following me around the room, making my blood heat and my core ache with longing.

There's no denying this attraction between us. No one looks at someone like that if they're not interested.

Every time I feel his eyes on me, my panties dampen and butterflies flutter behind my ribcage. Travis has had this butterfly effect on me ever since I was eighteen years old.

To think that he might like me back has my heart singing in all sorts of ways.

A cheer goes up from the corner where the drunk men are. One of them has spilled his beer on the table, and it drips onto the floor.

With a sigh, I grab a cloth and head over to the table.

"Sorrrry."

The man has red eyes and he's slurring. He lurches toward me as I approach the table, and his hand rests on my shoulder.

"What's your name?"

His breath stinks of beer and I dart forward, trying to get out of his grasp. But I'm not quick enough. His hand slides down my back, and his hand cups my backside.

I freeze at the contact. It's supposed to be a part of the job, being occasionally groped by drunk men, but I've never been able to get used to it.

The sound of a bar stool scrapes behind me, and a moment later Travis is grabbing the guy by the shoulder. The drunk man stumbles sideways, the grin slipping off his face.

"Don't fucking touch her."

There's a hard edge to Travis's voice that I've never heard before. He doesn't give the man time to apologize before he swings his fist. It connects with the drunk's nose, and blood spurts everywhere.

"What the fuck, man?" The man clutches his nose as blood drips into his hipster beard.

"Get the fuck out of my bar and don't come back."

Travis's face is red, a vein throbs in his neck, and his eyes glow dangerously. I've never seen him like this before. He's wild in this moment, my protector, and God help me, my panties dampen at the sight of him.

I get out of the way of the men, sure there's about to be a brawl and powerless to stop the male energy that's flying around the room.

Arlo comes out from behind the bar and Kobe joins him, standing behind Travis. They're a formidable sight. Three big, burly ex-military mountain men and two of them wearing bikers' patches.

The two groups of men face each other, sizing each other up.

I glance at Hailey and she's standing anxiously at the side of the bar, her hand on her pregnant belly. I go to her and take her hand, ready to flee through the back door if things get heated.

Luckily, there's one in the group of drunks who's sober enough to see sense.

"Come on."

He herds his friends to the door, and as soon as they're out of the restaurant the tension drops from the room.

"Are you okay?" Travis strides to where I'm standing with Hailey, the fire in his eyes still burning and making my knees weak.

I nod. "It was just a butt squeeze." I try to make light of it, but my words make Travis growl with anger.

"No one touches you." The possessiveness of his words make me shudder in a good way. But he's probably this protective of all his staff.

He lifts his hand to run it through his hair, and there's blood smeared across his knuckles.

"You're bleeding."

He winces as he flexes his fist. I don't know if it's his blood or the drunk man's.

"We need to get this disinfected. Where's the first aid kit?"

"My office."

I grab his wrist and lead him out the back and into the office. My heart's racing from the contact and what just went down. Travis stood up for me and took that asshole out.

I find the first aid kit and pull out a disinfectant wipe to mop up the blood. Then I get another one to clean out the cut.

"This might hurt."

I dab disinfectant on his cut, but he doesn't even wince.

"Tough guy, huh?"

Travis smiles. The fire has gone out of his eyes, and he's back to the affable guy I know.

"You can't be in the military and then cry over a minor cut."

It's not just a minor cut. The knuckles are turning purple, and they'll be bruised tomorrow.

"I'm gonna bandage this up for you. You need to rest it."

"Yes, doctor."

I glance at him, and he's smiling at me. My gaze darts

to his lips, and I look down quickly before I do something stupid like kiss him.

"Why'd you leave the military anyway?"

I haven't seen Travis since he spent Thanksgiving with us six years ago. It was soon after that that my parents passed away and I hit the road. I heard from Quentin that he was back, but I could never bring myself to see him until now.

"My time was done, and I was needed back here." He gives me a funny look I can't interpret. "Where have you been for the last six years anyway?"

It's my turn to be evasive. "Here, there, everywhere. The east mostly. Seasonal work in Kentucky and waiting tables in South Carolina."

Anywhere I could get away from the memory of my parents is what I don't add.

"What brought you back to the mountain?"

You, is what I want to say. It's been six damn years since I saw him, and he still plagues my dreams every night. No other man has ever lived up to Travis. I came back to see if I still felt the same, hoping that I wouldn't so I could move on with my life.

"To see if it felt like home yet."

He tilts his head. "You gonna stay?"

"That depends." I finish wrapping his hand and secure the bandage. Our heads are inches apart, and my heart's beating so loud he must hear it.

"On what?"

"If there's anything worth staying for."

There. I've said it in the most obvious way short of telling him I came back for him.

We stare at each other, our faces inches apart. I can't breathe.

Travis reaches his good hand up and cups my chin. He leans forward, and my lips part. I've been waiting for this kiss my whole damn life, and as he presses his lips to mine, all thought flies out the window. His lips are firm and warm and *hungry*.

His fingers grasp my neck, pulling me toward him and making my entire body light up. A moan escapes my lips. This is everything I ever dreamed of. Everything my schoolgirl self ever wanted.

The sound of the door to the restaurant swinging open has us jumping apart.

"You seen the mop?" Arlo asks as he swings his body around the office doorframe.

"Yeah." Travis's voice is tight with irritation. "In the cleaning cupboard."

"Not there, boss."

Travis sighs and heads for the door. He glances back at me, and his eyes are lit up like fire. "I'll be back in a minute."

He leaves the office with Arlo and I touch my lips, loving the way they tingle from his touch. A smile creeps across my face.

The kiss was better than I imagined. All these years, I've waited for Travis to kiss me. I've not let another man get close. I'm a twenty-four year old virgin. Stupid I know, but I've saved myself for him, for the only man I've ever wanted to touch me.

It seemed too easy to give it to someone else. I thought I'd meet someone who made me feel the way Travis does. But after working plenty of bars, I haven't met anyone I want to be intimate with.

Buzz Buzz

Travis's phone vibrates from the table where it's sitting.

A text from my brother lights up the screen.

You're keeping an eye on Kendra, right?

I want a full report.

I stare at the words, and my chest tightens. Travis has only been so attentive because Quentin asked him to be.

My stupid girlish fantasy got away from me. Thinking he's sitting at the bar watching me because he's attracted to me, but he's only watching me because my brother asked him to keep an eye on me.

He hit that guy not to stand up for me, but because Quentin wants a full report and he'll need to tell him what he did to protect his little sister.

And here I am throwing myself at him, practically begging him to kiss me.

Embarrassment prickles my skin. I've been so stupid.

I'm a silly girl who doesn't know a damn thing about men. I'm not going to stick around to embarrass myself anymore.

Grabbing my purse from the locker, I head upstairs to my room.

5

TRAVIS

The black waitress uniform hugs Kendra's luscious hips. The curve of her ass is a mouth-watering sight. I take another sip of my coffee, but it doesn't quench my thirst.

It's been over twelve hours since I kissed Kendra's pouty lips. But the taste of her lingers, filling up my senses. The imprint of her lips on mine, the memory of her teeth tugging my lower lip sends heat skittering over my body and blood thundering in my ears.

I thought I could resist Kendra. I thought this thing between us was stoppable. But now that I've had a taste, I realize how naïve I've been.

The pull I have towards her is overwhelming. It's bigger than her or me or her brother. I want to feel those lips on mine again, and to hell with the consequences.

I've been sitting here watching her work for the last two hours with my laptop open in front of me. I'm supposed to be doing inventory, but there's no way in hell I can keep my eyes off this woman.

I'm mesmerized by her, by the way she moves with the tray in the air, making her hips sway, the smile that lights up her face when she speaks to customers, that damn strand of bright pink hair that falls over her eyes and that she keeps tucking behind her ear.

I want to take that hair, wrap it in my fist, tilt her neck back, and kiss the hell out of her.

When I came back to the office last night, Kendra was gone. I don't know what I would have done if she'd still been there. Claimed her in the office, probably.

There was something between us last night, something real. But today, Kendra's barely said hello. She's avoiding me.

Does she regret kissing me last night? Does she regret kissing an old man? There's only one way to find out.

The last of the lunch customers leave, and Kendra clears their table and resets it for dinner.

There're a few hours before Kendra's needed for the night shift, and as she goes out to get her purse, I corner her in the hallway.

"Kendra."

She spins around and takes a small step back when she sees me, her hands going up as if pushing me away even as her eyes widen and her lips part.

My eyes dart to her plump lips, and my mind goes blank. All I can think about is kissing those peachy perfect creations.

"Did you want to see me?"

Her voice pulls me out of my fantasy, and I remember why we're here. "Get your coat."

Her eyes narrow, and she tilts her head. "Why?"

She doesn't trust me, or maybe she doesn't trust herself around me. The thought has my cock twitching.

"I'm taking you for a ride."

Her eyes go wide, and an adorable pink blush creeps up her neck. I chuckle, realizing what I just said.

"On my bike."

She turns away, embarrassed, and I love that her thoughts went to a dirty place.

"I haven't had lunch," she mumbles.

I know she hasn't, because I've been watching her all morning. While pretending to work, I've been following her every move. I can't help myself; I'm obsessed with this angel with the pink halo.

"I've packed a picnic." I hold up the bag of food I had Maggie prepare for me.

"Oh." Her mouth forms a perfect, dick-sized O, and I have to keep moving or she's going to notice the wood in my pants.

"Come on. I know a good spot."

She pulls her eyebrows together like she's going to protest, but I don't give her a chance. I grab her coat from the lockers and snatch the purse from her hands.

"Hey!"

She follows me down the corridor and out to the

bright sunshine of the courtyard. It's a beautiful, crisp spring afternoon, the perfect day for a ride.

"Are you always this bossy?" she asks when she catches up to me.

We reach my bike, and I stash the picnic in the saddle bags and help her shrug on her coat. "Only when there's something I want."

"Oh," she says again.

Pink creeps up her neck, and it's adorable how quickly I can make her blush. But she takes the helmet when I hand it to her.

Me and Quentin always had bikes growing up, and she's ridden with her brother before. But this is the first time I've felt Kendra on the back of my bike. Her thighs pressed against mine cause my nerves to go into overdrive.

She holds the side of the seat, and I pry them off and place them around my waist.

"Hold onto me. It's safer."

Which is bullshit, but if she's on my bike, her arms are around me.

We head onto the road, and it's pure bliss. The sun on my face, the bike humming beneath me, and Kendra on the back. Life doesn't get much better than this.

The road snakes uphill into the mountains. On one side, the cliff falls away to a canopy of trees and the commercial pine forest below. On the other side, it's a steep bank and wild forest.

After about twenty minutes, I take a dirt road that leads to one of my favorite walks on the mountain. Five minutes later, the dirt road doesn't end as much as peter out, the track giving way to undergrowth and scattered bush.

There's no one else here, and that's what I like about this spot. Most tourists go to the other side of the mountain where the town of Hope is. It's close to the lake and the ski fields and numerous hiking trails.

On the Wild side, we've got the sawmill and the forestry that feeds it, and beyond that pure wilderness.

The path isn't sign posted, and you won't find it on a tourist map. It's an old tracker path that only the locals know about.

Kendra slides off the bike and tugs the helmet off her head. She tosses her hair and runs her hands through it, letting the gold and pink locks fall back into place.

I must be staring, because she takes a strand of the pink and twists it in her fingers, making a face. "Pink seemed like a good idea in Kentucky."

"I like it."

I take the strand out of her fingers and tuck it behind her ear, loving the way she looks up at me all wide-eyed.

"Come on. The path's this way."

We set off through the undergrowth, and I pick up the faint track. As we walk, I probe Kendra about the last few years. I'm curious as to what she's been doing all this time and why she stayed away. As far as I know, Quentin's only seen her a handful of times when he visited her in whatever small town she was currently living in. I worried about her as much as he did.

"What were you doing in Kentucky?"

"Waitressing, mostly."

When I last saw Kendra, she had big dreams. She was going to go to college. She was going to study literature.

"What happened to college?"

"Life happened." She shrugs, and my heart breaks for her. For the innocent girl who's been through such pain.

We walk in silence for a while, listening to the noises of the forest. When Kendra speaks, she's so quiet I can barely hear her.

"After the accident, I couldn't focus. I didn't want to be away at college. It seemed so stupid, studying classic literature. What was the point? And all the stupid sororities and the drinking. I did one semester and gave up. I just didn't want to be there."

I can understand that. It was the same for me after the first tour in Iraq. When I came back and went into a bar and there were plenty of guys my age, young men getting wasted on tequila shots. It seemed so frivolous.

"You ever thought of going back to college?"

I want that for her. I want her to have her best life, not one that she fell into because of grief.

"Maybe, but not to study literature."

"You don't enjoy reading anymore?"

Kendra always had her head buried in a book. Romance mostly, judging from the bare-chested men on the covers.

She laughs. "Are you kidding? Reading has been what's gotten me through the last few years. But I want to do something more meaningful than write romance."

"What do you want to do?"

"I'd like to study psychology, be a therapist. Help people in some way."

She says it shyly, like it's the first time she's expressed her wishes out loud. I take her hand, and she glances at me but doesn't pull away.

"You'd make a great therapist. You should do it."

She bites her lower lip and smiles. "Maybe I will."

The conversation moves to other things.

Kendra asks me all about the bar and the MC club. And it seems like no time has passed before we reach the clearing.

There's a break in the canopy where sunlight filters in, and I spread the picnic blanket on the forest floor under the warm rays. Kendra plops down next to me, her short skirt riding up her thighs.

I grab the food and hand her a sandwich.

"You like chicken sandwiches?"

She takes it and we talk as we eat, the conversation flowing easily.

Maggie packed a large piece of apple pie and we share it, taking turns at scooping it up with a bamboo fork.

When we're done eating, Kendra lays back on the blanket and exhales deeply.

"I can see why you come here. It's peaceful."

Her hair fans out over the picnic blanket, and her eyes close.

I prop myself up on one elbow, drinking in the sight of her. For a long time, neither of us speaks. We listen to the bird sounds, and I watch her breathing.

One of her eyes peeps open and then narrows when she sees me watching her. "You don't have to take Quentin's instructions quite so literally."

I frown at her, not sure what she's talking about. "What do you mean?"

She props herself up on her elbows and looks at me.

"I know he told you to watch over me while he's away. And that's why you're in the bar when I'm working and why you've taken me out today."

Her words cut me. She thinks I'm only here because Quentin asked me to keep an eye on her.

"And I'm sorry I threw myself at you last night. It was silly. I was caught up in the moment…"

She trails off and looks down, a telltale blush creeping up her neck. She brings her arm up to smooth her hair, and I catch it in mid-air.

"Quentin's got nothing to do with it," I growl. "I brought you here because I want to spend time with you. And I kissed you last night because I've been wanting to kiss you for the last six years."

"Oh." Her mouth pops open. "So this has got nothing to do with my brother?"

At her mention of Quentin, I sit up and run my hand through my hair.

"No. The only worry about your brother is what he'd think if he knew how much I want to kiss his little sister."

She sits up, breathing hard, and crawls over to me. "Do you want to kiss me?"

From my position above her, I can see right down her T-shirt. Her chest heaves up and down as she breathes. My gaze darts to her plump lips, begging to be kissed.

"Yes." My voice sounds husky with desire. "I'd very much like to kiss you."

I grab her by the shoulders and press my mouth to hers. She moans as our lips collide.

She tastes like apple pie and cinnamon. Her body presses towards mine, and then I'm pushing her gently back onto the blanket.

She falls back and I pin her hand above her head, getting tangled in her hair.

"Kendra." I breathe her name into her neck, kissing her delicate skin, tasting her throat and neck and moving back to her waiting lips. "I've been wanting to do this for a very long time."

She moans as my hand slides over her tummy and up to her breasts, and I palm one as my finger flicks across her nipple.

"Travis…" Her voice comes out needy and small.

"What is it, angel?"

"Is this really happening? I've crushed on you since I was eighteen."

I smile at her confession, glad I'm not the only one who imagined this moment.

"Oh, it's happening, angel."

My lips find hers, and there's a new hunger to our kiss. Kendra's body writhes under me, and my hard-on bumps against her softness.

I've tasted her lips. Now I want to taste her most intimate places. My hand slides up her skirt, and she gasps as I reach her panties. My fingertips trail over the damp fabric.

"You're wet for me, angel."

She bites her bottom lip. "You have no idea."

My fingers pull aside her panties, and I brush against her sensitive folds.

The little gasps and moans that come out of her mouth make me wild with desire. But I'll take my time with her. I've waited so long for a taste of Kendra. Now I shuffle down on the blanket until my lips find the soft skin of her inner thigh.

"What are you doing?" Her head lifts off the blanket to look at me anxiously.

I give her a wicked smile. "I think you know exactly what I'm doing."

She bites her lower lip and gives me a cute look halfway between embarrassment and desire.

"Lie down," I tell her. "I'm going to take care of you."

"You're so bossy," she says. But she lies back on the blanket.

I slide her panties down her silky thighs and over her feet. Once I have them off, I bring them to my nose and inhale. The musky smell of her arousal makes my dick ache.

I stuff her panties in my pocket and dip my head between her thighs, throwing her skirt up to her waist. Kendra gasps as the cool air hits her pussy.

I sit back and look at her, my beautiful pink angel. Her hair is splayed out like a halo, and she's got a dreamy look in her eyes.

I put a hand on each thigh and push them apart. She opens up for me, revealing her perfect pink cunt.

"God, you're beautiful."

My hand stays on her pussy as I lower my head, and my lips brush her sensitive spot.

She bucks at the contact.

"Travis… "

I love the way she says my name, all whiny with need.

"What is, angel?"

"It feels too good. It's too much."

"Do you want me to stop?" I let my hot breath run over her pussy, and she shudders.

"No."

I chuckle. "Good. I'm not gonna stop until you scream my name."

My lips kiss her tender folds, and with every kiss she bucks her hips. Her nerves are pulled so tight, it won't take long to give her a release. Juice flows out of her pussy, and I press my tongue against her to lick her up.

She moans my name, and her hands clasp the back of my head.

Her pussy grows wetter as I lick and suck, keeping it slow and gentle, not quite giving her what she wants.

"Travis..."

It comes out as a whiny little whisper that drives me wild. Her hips buck, and she pulls my head towards her.

"Travis," she whines again, "what if someone comes?"

I lift my head and look around at the forest around us, the birdsong and the wind rustling the trees. Kendra's eyes meet mine, and they're full of desire and also anxious.

"Then I'll have to shoot them."

She giggles. But I'm only half joking.

I brought Kendra here because no one else knows about this spot. But if anyone saw this beautiful sight that I'm seeing now, I would have to kill them. No one sees my woman apart from me.

"Relax," I command, and she lies back on the blanket.

My thumb strums her clit as I slide my index finger into her tight little cunt. The walls of her pussy clench my finger. And she's so tight it makes me wonder if she's done this before. But that's a question I'll ask another time.

The thought thrills me. I want to be her first, and I want to be her last. But right now, I just want to make my angel come.

I slide my finger slowly in and out, loving the way she writhes under me. My tongue licks her clit, and I stretch my hand out until my pinky grazes her other little hole.

"Travis." She sits up in surprise, but there's desire in her look.

"Relax," I tell her. "I'm taking care of you."

She lays back down, and I go back to her sweet pussy. My tongue licks her from hole to hole and she grabs my hair, mewling my name.

"Keep saying my name, angel. I want you to say my name as you come. I want you to scream it. Let the entire forest know who's taking care of you."

She's panting hard, and I know it won't take me long now. I've drawn this out as long as I can, and as much as I love being down here, I want to give my girl a release. My speed picks up, strumming, sucking, licking, and finger fucking.

Her hips are bucking, and her hands are tugging at my hair. She writhes her hips, grinding her pussy into my mouth, and I push her hard, giving her everything she needs, licking her up and devouring her pussy like a mad man.

She screams my name as her pussy clenches, tugging at my fingers as juice cascades over my tongue.

I keep my mouth pressed to her, and just as she starts to come down, I start back up.

It doesn't take much to make Kendra come again. A little pressure from my mouth, a little twirl of my finger, and she's coming all over my tongue, grabbing my head with legs stuck straight up in the air.

She screams my name, and a flock of birds fly up from the trees and scatter into the sky.

But I don't let her rest. When one orgasm finishes, I move my mouth and she whimpers against me. I keep going, giving her everything she needs and more. Letting Kendra know I can look after her. That what she needs is an older man who knows how to take care of his woman.

I lose count of the number of times she comes, but finally her body goes limp. She lies back on the picnic blanket panting, her face sweaty and red and content.

"Travis." Every new way she says my name is a revelation. I thought screaming it as she came was the best, but whispering it in wonder comes pretty damn close. "I had no idea I could feel that good."

"Have something to drink, angel." I press the bottle of water to her lips, and she takes a few sips before collapsing back onto the blanket.

I take the panties out of my pocket and use them to mop up the pussy juice on her thighs. Then I stash them back in my pocket. They're coming home with me.

I lay down next to my angel.

"Kendra…"

There are so many questions I want to ask her. Is she sticking around? Can she ever be mine? But there's no response. My angel has fallen asleep.

6

KENDRA

The last two days have been the happiest of my life.

I've spent the days working at the restaurant and any spare time hanging out with Travis.

I was worried that he would think I was childish, still the teenage girl he knew before. But we talk easily about everything and anything. You don't notice the ten years' difference between us. Or at least, I don't.

We sneak off so the other guys in the MC suspect nothing. If my brother found out, he'd flip, and Travis doesn't want anyone telling him before he gets back.

I'm sure once Quentin sees how happy we are he'll be cool with us being together.

But it's not my brother I'm thinking of when Travis gets his wicked tongue on me. He does things with his mouth and hands that make me lose control in the best way. And I've learned to work his cock with my hands the way he likes. But we haven't gone all the way.

There's a niggling question in the back of my mind. I'm not experienced with men. I kept my distance when I was on the road. I don't know if what we're doing is casual or not. It doesn't feel casual to me, but what would I know?

We're finishing the washing up after the dinner he made, spaghetti and meatballs with a delicious homemade sauce.

Every night, Travis drops me at home under darkness so nobody sees. He says he's not ready to tell people yet. We have to tell Quentin first about us.

With the dishes all done, it's late and almost time to go. Travis leans on the kitchen counter.

"I guess I better drop you at home."

I'm not ready to go home yet. I take a step toward him, and he puts his arms around me, pulling me in close.

"Can I stay?"

Travis groans. "I would love for you to stay. But there's a way to do this. I can't disrespect your brother. I need to speak to him first."

I know it makes sense, but try telling my heart that.

I wiggle my hips against his, making him groan. My pussy dampens at the guttural noise coming from his throat. I'm not ready to go home just yet, and feeling bold, I pull my top off. His gaze roams hungrily over my breasts.

I pull his top off too and walk my fingers slowly down the hard muscles of his chest. When I get down to his belt, I slowly undo the belt buckle.

Travis has been taking care of me with his mouth. I want to return the favor.

"What are you doing, angel?" He growls a warning as I sink to my knees, sliding his belt out of its grooves.

"Oh, I think you know what I'm doing."

My hand runs over the bulge in his jeans, and I apply some pressure. Travis groans as I undo the zipper.

"You don't have to do that, angel."

"I know. I want to do it."

I slide his jeans and boxers over his hips and his cock pops out, hard and ready. I lick my lips at the glorious sight and push him back against the kitchen counter. My hands grip the base of his shaft and I hesitate, not sure what to do.

"I've never done this before."

His gaze meets mine, his eyes hooded with desire. "Have you done any of this before, Kendra?"

He means sex. Not that we've had penetration, but we've done a hell of a lot in the last few days. I shake my head.

"I was waiting for you, Travis." He groans, a tortured look on his face that makes me feel powerful, knowing I can bring a strong man to his knees. "I'm a virgin. I want you to be my first."

"Angel..."

It comes out as a low, tortured moan. A drop of

precum shoots out the end of his dick, and I duck my head and lick the pearly bead up with my tongue. His cock jerks my hands.

I glance up at him, wondering if I'm doing something right. Travis is watching me, and he gives an encouraging nod.

"You look good on your knees, angel. Take care of your man."

His words give me power, and I press my tongue to the base of his shaft and lick slowly upwards. He tastes salty and manly, and one lick gets my juices flowing.

My mouth experiments, licking and kissing his shaft and sliding my tongue around his tip. I slide him into my mouth, and his dick bumps up against my teeth. He's so big I have to slacken my jaw and stretch my mouth open wide. Even then, my mouth only comes halfway down his shaft.

I love watching his dick glisten as I take him in and out of my mouth. I glance upwards and Travis is watching me, his eyes dark with desire.

"That's it, angel. Take my cock into your mouth."

I keep sucking, loving his commands.

I suck and lick and tug and kiss. My teeth scrape against his skin, and it's sloppy and slobbery, but by the way he's moaning, I must be doing something right.

Then he grabs the back of my head. "Open your throat, angel."

He's bossing me around, and I like it. He grabs the back of my hair and slides my head down his shaft. I feel like my eyes are going to bug out of my head and I gag, but then I do as he says. My throat opens, and his cock grazes my tonsils.

He's in so deep, and when he groans with pleasure my pussy aches.

My jaw drops right open, and my lips rub up and down his shaft as he pulls my head up and down him. My fingers cup his balls and I slide one finger around to his back passage, playing with his puckered hole the way he does with mine.

"Fuck Kendra."

The surprise in his voice makes me wet and needy.

"That's it." His voice is strained and croaky. "Good girl, Kendra. Good girl."

I know I'm doing a sloppy job. It's my first time. But the way he's moaning makes me feel powerful.

His fist twists in my hair. Then he pulls my head down and suddenly he's got control. He's fucking my mouth, and it's so damn sexy.

I love that I'm pleasing him, even though it feels like my jaw is about to drop off. I keep going, sucking and licking and moving my head where he pulls me.

My tits are bouncing up and down, straining at my pink lacey bra. And he's watching them as he pulls himself into my mouth.

"You're so sexy, Kendra. So damn sexy. I'm gonna come all over your tits."

Oh god. It's so dirty that new heat floods my pussy,

and I'm aching for some friction down there but I've got both hands on his cock.

I feel his cock thicken. Then he rips it out of my mouth and grabs the base of his cock. Hot liquid hits my tits and splashes onto my face as he sprays cum on my chest.

Cum trickles over my skin and I'm panting, hot and wet. He sees my need and drops to his haunches, pulling me onto the wooden floor with him.

"You need taking care of, angel."

I whimper as he throws up my skirt and tugs my wet panties off. With his other hand, he swirls his cum all over my chest.

"You're mine."

The words only make me more needy. I find his cock, and he's already hard again.

"Fuck me, Travis," I whimper.

For the last two days we've fooled around a lot, but we haven't been all the way. Now I'm crazy with desire and want his cock in me.

He growls. But he doesn't give me what I need.

His cock presses against my thigh, and it's so fucking close.

"No, angel. I won't claim you yet."

Disappointment courses through me, and I grab his cock and pull it towards me.

But his hand gets there first. He thrusts two fingers into my dripping pussy. I'm so needy that it only takes two pumps before I come on his palm.

The release is intense and I press myself to him, our bodies covered in each other's juices. He moves his fingers again and I tug his cock. Then he's coming with me, hot cum squirting onto my thigh.

I give a frustrated cry. I want him in me so bad.

"Not yet, Kendra." He kisses me gently. "I will claim you soon. I will take that sweet cherry of yours, but you have to be patient, angel. This has to be done right."

He's thinking of my brother again and what Quentin would do to him if he found out what Travis has been up to with his little sister. It makes sense to wait, but I don't see how coming on my tits is any less disrespectful than making love.

But I'm too tired to argue. Travis scoops me up and takes me to his bedroom. He washes me down with a warm flannel and climbs into bed next to me.

Every night, he's taken me back to the clubhouse on his bike. But tonight we sleep together, wrapped tight in each other's arms.

7
TRAVIS

Kendra sleeps like she comes, all in. Her hair's spread over the pillows, her mouth hangs open emitting soft snores, her legs are tangled in the bed sheets, and she's taking up way more than half the bed.

A feeling of contentment spreads over me as I watch her. I could get used to this.

It's only been a few days that we've been together, but it's been a lifetime that I've wanted this woman.

She's frustrated because we haven't gone all the way, but we've got a lifetime together. Why rush? Besides, I need to speak to Quentin first, out of respect for my best friend and MC brother.

And there's something else I want to do. I want Kendra to know how serious I am. While she's working today, I'm taking a ride across the mountain to Hope.

There's a boutique jewelry shop there, and I'm going to buy her a ring.

I don't want her running off again. I want her to be here, tied to me as my fiancé. Once I've got a ring on her finger, I'll tell her brother. Then I'll claim her. And I'll put a baby in her belly and keep her tied to me for good.

Kendra stirs and I hate to wake her, but I need to drop her back at the club while it's still early. I hate sneaking around like this, but it's only for one more day, and the last thing I want is the rumor mill starting before I've spoken to Quentin.

I slip out of bed and get the coffee going, then wake up my angel with a fresh brew.

"Morning, angel."

Kendra grunts and sits up in bed, reaching for the coffee with her eyes half closed. She's not a morning person.

Dawn's breaking over the crest of the mountain as we ride to the compound. As soon as she's got a ring on her finger, she'll be staying at my place permanently. But for now, I return her to the room above the bar.

Kendra heads upstairs, probably to go back to sleep, while I head to the office.

I spend the next few hours catching up on inventory, my mind wandering to Kendra and making it hard to focus. I wonder if I'll stop obsessing about her once we're engaged and I know she's mine.

The morning shift comes in, and I chat with Arlo. Maggie walks past, and I notice his eyes following her.

She's proving indispensable in the kitchen, and I hope he doesn't do anything to make her want to leave. It's hard enough finding staff to stick around.

Kendra comes down to start her lunch shift. She's had a shower and her hair is tied back off her face, which is radiant. She smiles at me, and I resist the urge to kiss her.

Soon. Soon I'll let every motherfucker in this place know that she's mine. But not till I've told Quentin first.

I'm about to take my laptop out to the bar so I can keep an eye on Kendra when I hear the roar of bikes pulling into the compound. I head to the window as four Wild Riders pull into the courtyard. It's Quentin and Prez and the two other guys who went with them. I frown. They're not meant to be back for two more days.

Two more days that I had to convince Kendra to marry me and stay on the mountain.

The phone rings in the office, and I head back inside. It's a query about one of our orders, and I deal with it quickly. I'm about to hang up when Quentin appears in the door frame.

"Hey, brother."

He's staring at me, and I wonder if there's some way that he knows. Me and Kendra have been discreet, but maybe someone saw us. Then he slaps me on the back and grins.

"You're back early. What happened?"

Quentin fills me in on the meetings they had with new distributors and the ones that were cancelled because of flooding in the area. Entire roads were closed, and they cut their losses and came back. We'll have to arrange the meetings for another time.

With business talk out the way, Quentin pulls on his beard and looks at me intently. "How's Kendra? Anything I need to know?"

8
KENDRA

*M*y stomach twists at the sound of bikes roaring into the compound. Quentin's back. Travis will tell him about us, and we can stop sneaking around. Our relationship will be public, and I won't have to get up at some godawful time in the morning just so no one sees us.

"Could you grab me some more napkins?" Arlo asks.

He's been on every shift with me and Travis and must know there's something between us, but he keeps his expression neutral, and I hope he's discreet long enough for Travis to speak to Quentin first.

I check the station, and we're all out of napkins.

"I'll get some from out back." It's a quiet shift, and they won't miss me for a moment.

The supply closet is down the corridor next to the office, and as I approach, I hear the low rumble of Quentin and Travis talking.

Butterflies beat in my chest. What if they're talking about me? I shake the thought out of my head. It's their conversation to have in private. Opening the door to the supply cupboard, I grab the napkins and shut it quietly.

I'm about to head back to the restaurant when I hear my name.

"How's Kendra?" asks Quentin.

I pause to listen. It's not eavesdropping if you're the topic of conversation, right?

"Anything I need to know about?"

I clutch my throat as the butterflies inside me beat against my chest. This is the moment that Travis tells my brother about us. That he tells him we're in love and we're going to be together. Then Quentin will slap him on the back and tell him he always wanted him to be part of the family. They'll have a beer together and Travis will kiss me in front of his club, claiming me as his old lady. And all my teenage fantasies will come true.

Except that's not what Travis says. "She's doing okay," he says.

My heart stops beating for a moment.

She's doing okay.

What the hell does that mean? I was doing more than okay. When I had his cock in my mouth last night, he was singing my praises like I was a goddess.

"Nothing to report," says Travis.

"Thanks for keeping an eye on her," Quentin says. "I know it can't have been fun watching my kid sister."

Travis mumbles something that I can't make out. But I've heard enough.

Nothing to report.

He was supposed to tell Quentin about us. Tell him we love each other and want to be together. Unless that's not what he wants? He's never said those words. We've messed around, and he's told me I'm sexy and beautiful and made me come so many times I lost count. But he's never told me this is forever.

The reality comes crashing down on me. I've been so stupid. I'm his best friend's kid sister. My stupid teenage fantasies have run away with me again.

Of course Travis wouldn't be interested in a pink-haired girl who's barely out of her teens. He was tasked with babysitting me and thought he'd have some fun along the way. That's why he didn't want anyone to see us. That's why he didn't want to go all the way. Because this isn't some teenage romance. This is real life, and in real life, men suck.

I've been so stupid. I shouldn't have come back.

There's movement in the office, and I quickly dart out of the way.

I take the door at the end of the corridor that leads upstairs. Going quickly and quietly, I throw off my apron and chuck it over the end of the bed. My stuff doesn't take long to pack. Then I sling my duffel bag over my shoulder and take the fire escape that leads to the side of the courtyard. Nobody sees me as I drop to the ground.

I keep to the shadows until I'm past the compound.

Then I walk quickly down the mountain road away from the restaurant, away from the Wild Riders MC, and away from Travis.

It's a few miles to Wild where I can get a bus to Hope and then a train to wherever the hell gets me out of here the quickest. Unless I get a ride first. Once I get around the corner, I stick out my thumb.

Life on the road is uncomplicated. There's only myself to look out for and no stupid heart to get in the way. It was a mistake to come here.

9
TRAVIS

As Quentin talks to me about the meetings, my mind becomes more agitated. I don't enjoy lying to him about Kendra. The sooner I can get out of here and buy her the ring, the better. I'm about to make my excuses when Arlo comes in from the bar.

"You guys seen Kendra?"

At the sound of her name, my head jerks up. There's a tone to Arlo's voice that I don't like.

"She's in the restaurant, isn't she?"

Arlo shakes his head. "She went to get napkins twenty minutes ago, and I haven't seen her since."

I glance at Quentin, and he's scowling at Arlo.

"What do you mean you haven't seen her?"

"She didn't come back to finish her shift. It's not like her."

Kendra's only been working at the restaurant for a

week, but she's reliable. I push my chair back and stand up, my heart hammering in my chest.

"She might be upstairs."

Quentin and I both bolt for the door, and I get there just ahead of him. I take the stairs two at a time and race to her room.

"Kendra." I bang on her door, and there's no answer. "Kendra!"

I push the door open and barge in. Her waitress apron lies on the bed, along with the branded t-shirt and black skirt that makes up her uniform.

"Shit."

I pull open the closet, and it's empty.

Quentin barges into the bathroom, but our search of the room reveals what my heart already knows. "She's gone."

I can't keep the despair out of my voice. I thought we had something real. I thought she felt the same about me as I do about her. I don't know why she would run.

Quentin tugs on his beard and turns his intense gaze on me.

"Why would she leave?"

I drag my gaze around the room, not wanting to meet his eye. I can't lie to him anymore.

"Travis…" His voice has a rough edge to it. "Why would Kendra leave?"

I meet his gaze, and his eyes are dark with suspicion. I suck in a deep breath and let it out slowly. I've got to tell him.

"Is there something I need to know, Travis?"

Quentin takes a step towards me. They don't call him Barrels for nothing. It's not only because he runs the brewery. The man's thick and stocky, built like a barrel.

I put my hand up in the air in a placating gesture.

"It's not what you think."

That's the wrong thing to say. Because Quentin's expression goes from suspicion to fury in two seconds flat.

"What the fuck, man? Have you been fucking my sister?"

I wince at the harsh words. "It's not like that."

"So something is going on between you?"

He tugs at the side of his mouth and jostles his feet. I know what's coming before he swings the punch. I dodge his fists, and he comes at me again.

"Fuck you, man. She's my sister."

He lunges at me and we go barreling into the dresser, bringing the mirror crashing to the ground.

"It's not like that."

We tumble to the floor, and I roll away out of his grasp.

Quentin is a big guy, and I'm faster than him so I can dodge his fists, but I won't fight back. If he hits me, then I fucking deserve it. This is a shitty thing to do to your best friend.

I scramble to my feet and Quentin faces me, breathing hard.

"I love her, man."

His eyes narrow.

"I don't give a shit. You don't touch my sister." He comes at me again and I dodge out the way, but he clips my shoulder. A flash of pain shoots down my arm, and I stagger backwards.

"I love her." I say it louder. And it feels damn good to say it.

Quentin swivels around and swings at me again, and I dive under his arm and skip backwards across the room.

"Listen to me, Quentin. I love Kendra. I'm going to marry her. I was waiting for you to get back to tell you."

"You want to marry Kendra?"

The talk of marriage stops him. He's breathing hard, bent over with his hands on his knees, and we stare at each other across the room.

He's like a raging bull, and I don't know if he's going to charge. I don't give him a chance.

"I tried to deny my feelings, man. But I love her. She's the most amazing, smart, funny, kind, caring woman I've ever met. I want to make her my wife. I want to do right by her."

He's breathing heavily as he stares at me, the words sinking in.

We've been through a lot of together, me and Quentin. We fought alongside each other; we've seen shit a man shouldn't see. We've been through hell and back, and we've ridden together to chase the demons out of our lives.

It's only because he knows me so well that I'm still standing right now.

"She feel the same way about you?"

My shoulders sag with relief that he's coming around to the idea.

"I don't know," I say honestly. "I hope so. I was going to buy her a ring today and find out. I'm not messing around with her, Quentin. This is for keeps."

"This is a lot take in." He lets out a big sigh and runs his hands through his hair.

"But if she loves you, why the fuck has she gone?"

His words have me racing for the door. "I don't know. But I'm gonna find her and find out."

We've wasted time fighting and Kendra could be miles away, picked up in some stranger's car. The thought has me bolting down the stairs.

I hear Quentin running behind me as I sprint to my bike.

"I'm coming too. I don't know what the fuck has gone on between you two, but if she's running away from you, it can't be fucking good."

His words have a grim warning to them. I wanted to get his blessing, but we're a long way from that.

I push the thought out of my head as I gun the engine. I can't let Kendra leave the mountain. I have to find her.

10
KENDRA

There's a blister forming on my left heel. I should put my sneakers on, but in my haste to get the hell away from the Wild Riders clubhouse, I pulled on my knee-high boots. The heel on them means they're not made for walking long distances, but in the half hour I've been on the road, I've seen only two cars.

These remote mountain roads aren't good for hitchhikers.

The goddamn birds are singing too loud and the sun blasts my face, making me squint. But I can't waste time stopping to get my sunglasses out of my bag. I want to put as much distance between me and Travis as possible.

How could I be so stupid as to think there was anything real between us? It's my stupid teenage fantasies where we get together and live happily ever after messing with my head. I thought I was playing them out, but he was just playing with me.

I don't think Travis meant to play me. He's an older man and probably has affairs with women all the time. I'm just too inexperienced with men to realize that's all it was.

Travis never promised me anything. It was all me that put that on us, wanting to believe in my teenage fantasy.

But that just makes it harder. If Travis was an asshole, at least I could feel angry. But all I feel is a deep sadness, a heaviness in my chest. It's a heaviness that makes it hard to put one blistered foot in front of the other. It'll take me another hour to get to town. And then I'm changing shoes, getting on the bus, and never coming back.

An engine roars somewhere behind me, and I step to the side of the road and stick my thumb out, waiting for the car to come around the corner.

But it's not a car. It's a motorbike, and it screeches to a halt beside me, kicking up gravel and dust into my eyes.

"I thought I told you not to hitchhike."

Travis slides off his bike and saunters toward me like a protective big brother. Still watching out for me like Quentin asked him to.

I drop my bag in the dirt and put my hands on my hips. Now I'm glad I'm wearing my knee high boots because they make me look like a tough bitch, even though inside I feel like a silly schoolgirl in love.

If he's come to lecture me, I won't show him any vulnerability.

But as he strides over to me, the concern in his eyes

almost makes me crumble. Almost. I remember the words that he said to Quentin.

Nothing to report.

I'll give him nothing to report. He'll know nothing of my feelings. I stick my chin out, ready to go into battle, but instead he cups it in his hand and pulls my face toward his. I'm speechless as his thumb strokes my cheek. "Don't leave, Kendra."

His eyes search mine, and my resolve crumbles. The tears I've been fighting back bubble to the surface and I squeeze my eyes shut, not wanting him to see how much I'm hurting.

"Don't go, Kendra," he says. "I want you to stay."

With my eyes squeezed shut, I can't see his face. I think about everything that's gone on between us. His reluctance to go all the way, the sneaking around so no one sees, and then not telling my brother when he had the chance. Anger bubbles to the surface, and I pull away and out of his grasp.

"So you can keep sneaking around with me as your fuck buddy?"

He stumbles backwards as if I've slapped him.

"No, it's not like that."

"Isn't it? Because it feels like you're embarrassed to be with me."

He's got a horrified expression on his face, and he's shaking his head.

"No. Kendra, you can't think that."

Another bike rolls around the corner, and Quentin

comes into view. He slams on the brakes and pulls up behind us. He's off the bike and striding over, not bothering to take his helmet off.

"Are you fucking hitchhiking?"

I roll my eyes at my over-protective big brother. "It's the quickest way to get off this damn mountain."

Travis flinches at the words and looks wounded.

"Is it because of this asshole?" Quentin stands between us and jerks his thumb at Travis. I've never seen him angry at his best friend before. "He tells me he loves you, but there's got to be a reason you're leaving. If he's done anything to hurt you, I swear to God I will ruin that pretty face of his."

Quentin paces in anger, and as he talks he points an angry finger at Travis. But my brain got stuck when he used the "L" word.

My gaze darts to Travis and he's staring at me, his expression hurt and anxious.

"It's true. Angel, I love you. I'm not sneaking around because I'm embarrassed. It's because I respect your brother, and I wanted his blessing. But I see now that was a mistake. I love you, Kendra. I always have."

He takes my hand, and my resolve melts away. Our eyes lock and I search his, looking for the truth.

Quentin growls.

"Is this what you want, Kendra? Is this really what you want? If he's forced himself on you, if he's hurt you in any way... I don't care if he's my best friend. He'll be off this mountain and out of your life with a broken face."

I look between both men. Both of them showing their love for me in different ways. My heart fills with joy at how lucky I am. To have these two men looking out for me, my overprotective brother and the man I love, with a code of honor that I don't understand.

"Yes. That's what I want."

Travis reaches behind me and snaps a pine needle from a tree.

"This isn't how I was planning it, but I want you both to know how serious I am."

He drops to his knees in the gravel as he twists the pine needle into a circle. I gasp as I realize what he's about to do.

Travis glances at Quentin who's as wide-eyed as I am.

"Could you give us a moment here, man?"

Quentin steps back, and Travis turns back to me.

"Kendra, I've loved you since the day I turned up for Thanksgiving at your house. I've carried your photo in my wallet for the last six years. It's your face I turned to during the dark times. When I was in Iraq and it felt like hell, I would pull out that photo and think of you. Sorry if my stupid honor kept me from doing this sooner. I was gonna buy a ring today, but if this is what I have to do to get you to stay on the mountain, then this will have to do. Will you make me the most fulfilled man alive and marry me?"

The butterflies explode out of my chest and come rushing out in a joyful, "Yes!"

I throw my arms around Travis, and he spins me around and around until I'm dizzy. He sets me down on the ground, and there's a broad grin on his face.

We're both laughing, and I glimpse Quentin watching us with a frown.

"Do I have your blessing?" Travis asks.

Quentin runs his hand through his hair. "It's a lot to get used to. I need some time. But if my sister has to marry someone, I guess I'm glad it's you."

Knowing my brother, that's about the biggest blessing we're ever going to get.

Travis slaps him on the back. "Thanks, man."

Suddenly, my feet lift off the ground as Travis scoops me into the air. I throw my arms around his neck as he kisses me hard.

Quentin scowls. "You're not married yet."

I throw him a look. "Can you take my bag? There's no room on the bike for it."

Quentin shakes his head and mumbles curses. But he picks up the bag and straps it to the back of his bike as I take my place behind Travis.

"Are we going back to work?"

"No." He shakes his head. "We're going to my cabin. You've been driving me crazy all week, Kendra. It's time to claim what's mine."

A shiver of anticipation goes through my body. The

vibration of the bike rumbles under me, and heat gushes between my legs as we race back up the mountain. I am ready to be claimed.

11
TRAVIS

Dust from the road kicks up behind us as we speed up the mountain. I'm breaking every speed limit in the county, but I've got my girl, no, my fiancé behind me, and I'm not slowing down for anyone.

Kendra's arms are tight around me, and she rests her head on my back. Her body's pressed against mine, warming me up and filling me with anticipation of what's to come.

As soon as we pull up in front of my cabin, I cut the engine. She slides off the bike, and I lift her into my arms.

Kendra squeals, and her arms go around my neck. Her girlish giggle makes me feel like a young man again, energized and full of hope instead of hardened by war. I love that she makes me feel like that.

I unlock the cabin with one hand and carry her inside, kicking the door shut behind us.

"Hey, I've got a shift to finish." She wiggles in my arms.

"Nope. Not today."

The restaurant will have to cope without us for a few hours, because I've got plans for Kendra. I carry her into the bedroom and sit her down on the edge of the bed.

"I don't want people to think I'm getting special treatment because I'm sleeping with the boss."

She's teasing me, giving me some sass, and I love it. But before she can say anything else I press my mouth to hers, quieting that sassy mouth for a while.

I put my hands on her thighs and sit back, crouching on the floor before her.

"That sassy mouth is going to get you in trouble one day."

She gives me a cheeky smile. "I hope so."

The look she's giving me makes all the blood rush to my dick. I've had a permanent hard-on ever since she walked into my bar, and now it's time to do something about it.

Kendra's wearing sexy knee-high boots, and as I crouch between her thighs, the leather scrapes my skin, sending heat coursing through my body, and dirty ideas spring into my mind.

She leans forward to unzip her boot, and I stop her hand.

"These are staying on."

Her mouth pops open, and I chuckle as her surprised look turns to curiosity. I slide a hand up her skirt and caress the gusset of her panties. They're dripping wet, and the moan that escapes her lips lets me know how ready she is for this.

"You're wet for me. Good girl."

"I've been wet for you ever since I was eighteen." She leans back on the bed, propped up by her elbows. "All I ever wanted was for you to take my cherry."

She bites her bottom lip and gives me an innocent look like she's that eighteen year old girl again.

"Keep talking, angel. Tell me about that teenage fantasy of yours."

She bows her head and peeps out at me from lowered lashes.

"You might think I'm silly."

"I doubt that, angel. You're sexy as hell." My fingers brush her panties, and she gasps. "Now tell me the fantasy."

She smiles. "You're as bossy in my fantasies as you are in real life."

"Oh yeah? What do I tell you to do?"

She bites her lower lip, and she takes a while to get the words out. It's not until I press my thumb against her panties and rub her clit that she opens her mouth.

"First, you tell me to take my panties off." Her voice comes out breathless, and the more she talks the harder I get.

I hook my thumbs under the top of her panties, and she lifts her hips so I can slide them off. She sticks her legs out, and I take them right over the top of those sexy leather boots and drop them on the floor.

"Then what?" My voice comes out raspy. But I'm so turned on by her teenage fantasy, to know this is what she wanted and now I can give it to her.

"Then you would tell me to undress."

I tug at her skirt until it's on the floor. Then I pull her t-shirt over her head. Her perfect breasts are bursting out of a pink lacy bra. She's a vision, leaning back on the bed with nothing but her bra and boots on. But I want to see more. I want to see all of her.

"Take your bra off, angel."

I set an edge to my voice to make it commanding, and a shiver goes through her. I sit back on my haunches to watch her undress herself.

Her hands slip around and unhook the bra and she crosses her arms and eases the straps off her shoulders, pulling the bra slowly off until her beautiful round globes are free.

Just the sight of those pink nipples standing on end has me hard as a rock. I want to plunge myself between those breasts. I want to run my dick over every part of this woman. But I'm a patient man, and I'm enjoying this exquisite torture.

"What happens next in your fantasy, angel?"

She gives me a shy smile. "Then I touch myself."

Her hand slides over her body and snakes up to her breasts. She cups a tit in one hand, and her thumb brushes over the nipple. She's biting her bottom lip, and as she works her nipple, her look turns from uncertainty to pure desire.

This may be a teenage girl's fantasy, but Kendra's all woman now.

"Now what?" I'm breathing hard, and I've never been so turned on.

"Then you touch me."

I bring my hand back to her pussy, and my fingers graze her sticky folds. But she shakes her head. The embarrassed girl is gone, and in front of me is a confident woman who knows what she wants.

"With your mouth."

I don't have to be told twice. I duck between her legs and hoist one thigh over my shoulder. The leather boot brushes against my skin, sending shivers all through me. My mouth presses to the soft skin of her leg just above the boot.

She gives a little whimper, and I look up.

"Keep playing with those gorgeous tits, angel. And don't stop until you're screaming my name."

She gasps at my command, but the good girl does as she's told.

I kiss her inner thigh, taking my time and enjoying the taste of her.

The closer I get to her musky core, the harder my heart pounds. With one hand I unzip my cock, needing to let the beast out.

"This is all for you, angel. You're gonna ride my cock in a minute. But first, I'm gonna get you warmed up."

My mouth goes back to the top of her thigh, inching towards her sticky core. She pushes her hips forward, trying to hurry me along. But I'm enjoying taking my time and making her squirm.

Finally, my lips brush her pussy opening and she whimpers. She's glistening wet, and I lick up all her juices as she quivers against me.

I glance up, and she's looking down at me as her hands tweak her nipples. I take my hand off my cock and I slide it between her folds, getting my finger nice and coated in pussy juice. Then I slide it into her.

She cries out and bucks her hips forward, taking every part of my finger. Her tight little pussy opens for me. In a moment, I'll have my cock in there. The thought drives me wild, and I plunge my fingers into her as I lick and suck. She throws her other leg over my shoulder, and leather rubs against the skin of my neck.

She shuffles her hips down the bed so that her legs wrap around me and the heels of her boots dig into my shoulders. I gasp as pricks of pain shoot through my body and straight to my dick. Precum spurts out of me, and I'm about to lose it without even getting inside her.

I roll my tongue over her clit, licking and sucking. She's panting hard, and then she's screaming my name as her pussy convulses.

I don't give her a chance to come down. I need to be inside Kendra, and I need it now.

I stand up and pull my jeans and boxers down in one movement.

Then I'm standing above her with my dick pointing straight at her tight little cunt. It's dripping and it's throbbing, and she licks her lips and edges forward, but I push her back.

"I'm getting inside that tight little pussy, angel, and I'm making you mine. I'm clean, and I'm not using a condom."

She nods. "Okay."

"Good. Because I'm gonna put my baby in your belly and tie you to me forever."

I climb between her thighs, and she scrambles back on the bed. I push her backwards and she bounces with the force of it, making her tits bump together. I lie on top of her, forcing her thighs apart with my legs. I'm being rough, but I can't stop.

My cock is taking over. I've seen her tight little cunt, that pink hole looking so inviting, and there's nothing I can do now to stop it.

"This might hurt for a minute, angel."

My gaze meets hers. It's taking all my restraint to hold back, but I need to let her know how I feel before I totally destroy her.

"I love you, Kendra." Emotion wells up inside me as I say it. She opens her mouth to speak, but I don't give her a chance. I thrust hard into that tiny little hole.

She screams and her thighs clutch me, the leather brushing my skin and driving me wild. I stay still inside her as her pussy clenches around me, and she's so tight it feels like she might squeeze my cock right off. Her eyes are shut tight, and I can't have that.

"Look at me, Kendra."

Her eyes open, and she holds my gaze as I slowly inch out of her. My cock's covered in her virgin blood and glistening juices.

"I love you. But I'm going to destroy you."

I pull my hips back and I thrust again, needing to pound this pussy. Needing to take out all my years of frustration, all the waiting, all the longing.

She had her youthful fantasies, but I had mine, and now I'm living them out as I pound into Kendra, her body bouncing like a rag doll with every thrust.

"I've imagined this for so long, angel."

Fucking my palm, thinking about her pussy, and now that I'm in her I'm like a man possessed.

But I want to go deeper.

I pull out, and she whimpers.

"Get on your knees."

She does as she's told like a good girl, and I kneel behind her and grab her hips.

My cock runs over her puckered back hole. One day soon I'll claim that too, but not today. Today I need the pussy I've been dreaming about for all these years.

I grab her ass and tilt her hips upwards, and there it is. Her pink pussy. So fucking gorgeous.

My cock twitches at the sight of her glistening hole, and I'm about to thrust into her when she surprises me by moving her hips back, sinking herself down my shaft.

A groan escapes me, and she moans at the same time. "Fuck, Kendra."

I'm lost for words. I can't speak. The sensation is too great. I pull her back and forth down my cock, my thrusts getting harder and faster. She's bouncing up and down and the bed is jumping about and the springs can't last, but I can't be gentle. I can't slow this down; my need is too great.

My dick plunges in and out of her as my thumb brushes against her puckered asshole.

"Touch yourself."

I love commanding her, and like a good girl, she obeys.

Her hand reaches between her legs and she rubs her clit, her fingernails brushing against my balls. "Good girl, Kendra."

She glances over her shoulder, and her gaze meets mine.

My God, this woman means so much to me. In that look, I see love. I see my future. I see everything that's good in this world.

"Come for me, angel."

Her eyes go wide, and her pussy clenches around me as she screams my name. My cock thickens and the animal inside me takes over and I'm fucking her so hard that her head's hitting the headboard. "Fuck, fuck, FUCK Kendra!"

Cum erupts out of me, and my entire body seems to explode. Thick ropes of seed slam into her pussy and I thrust, and I thrust, and I thrust until I'm spent. Everything I've saved up for her for the last six years, I let her have it.

When I pull my cock out of her, it's coated in her virgin blood and my sticky cum.

She flops down on the bed, and I collapse next to her. Only now does she slip off those goddamn sexy leather boots.

"My God, Travis." She's breathless. "That was unreal. Is it always like that?"

I pull her close to me and plant little kisses on her head.

"It's however we want to make it, angel. I had six years of cum, six years of waiting built up inside me that I had to give you. You'll hurt tomorrow, but next time I'll be gentler. I promise."

She gives me that shy smile. "What if I don't want it gentle?"

My cock hardens at her words.

"Angel, you can have it any way you want. We've got an entire lifetime to figure it out."

She nestles against me, content and happy, and her breathing soon becomes regular as she falls into sleep.

I pull the blanket over the both of us and hold her close. I got everything I ever wanted, and it's so much more than I ever expected.

EPILOGUE

KENDRA

One year later...

The scowl on Travis's face lets me know I'm in trouble even before he opens his mouth.

"I told you not to work today, angel."

I sling the apron over my head defiantly. The tie at the back almost doesn't come together over my round belly, but I manage to secure it.

"Jeez, Travis. It's only pregnancy. I can still work."

He rubs my belly. "I'd prefer it if you didn't."

"You're short on staff. It's a quiet lunch shift. I'm just going to wait a few tables for a couple of hours. There's nothing to worry about."

He looks uncertain. But then Maggie calls out a food order, and I give him a kiss on the cheek and waddle off before he can tell me off again.

It's sweet how protective Travis has been since I got

pregnant. But I wouldn't do anything to endanger the baby. I've cut my shifts back, not because of the pregnancy but because of my studies. I'm taking an online psychology course. It will be a few years of study doing it part time, but when I'm done, I'll be a qualified therapist.

With the scowl still on his face, Travis takes a seat at the bar. That's where he always works when I'm on shift. He says he thinks better there, but I know it's because he can keep an eye on me. My overprotective man. It makes me feel safe and cared for.

I'm taking a tray of drinks to a table when Quentin strides into the bar. He frowns at my stomach and takes the tray off me.

I give a long sigh.

"Jeez. Between the two of you, a girl can't do anything anymore."

He turns his frown on Travis. "What are you doing letting her work?"

Travis shrugs. "You ever try to stop your sister from doing something she really wants to do?"

Quentin still hasn't gotten used to the idea of us being together, even though we're married now.

We had a quiet ceremony in the Wild Chapel officiated by the Prez. With so many of his MC getting married, he got himself ordained.

It was our MC family and some of our friends from the other side of the mountain. I've gotten to know the people on Wild Heart Mountain and the small but tight community who lives here.

I just wish that Quentin would accept me and Travis. He gave me away at the wedding, but he's still coming around to the idea.

With both of them scowling at me, I know when I'm beaten.

"Fine," I say. "One of you wait the tables. I'm going to fold napkins."

I undo the apron and hold it out to my two protectors. Travis and Quentin look at each other.

Travis takes the apron and throws it on the bar. "I'll cover the shift, but I'm not wearing an apron."

The phone behind the bar rings, and I'm closest so I grab it.

"Wild Taste Bar and Restaurant, Kendra speaking."

It's Joseph on the other end. He's known as Lone Star to the MC club because of his hermit nature. Of all the guys at the MC, he's the one I know the least. He only comes in for the weekly meetings and prefers his own company up in the woods.

"Are Kobe and Hailey up there?" he asks.

I've gotten to know the loved up couple from the other side of the mountain. They stop by often, although not as much since they had the baby.

"I haven't seen them. Hang on and I'll double check."

I glance around the restaurant, peering into the corners and the eating area across the road. Travis gives me a questioningly look.

"Have Hailey and Kobe been in today?"

He shakes his head. "Who wants to know?"

"Lone Star."

He takes the phone off me and holds it so we can both hear.

"They're away for the weekend. Went to the coast."

I share a look with Travis. It's unusual for Lone Star to call.

"I went up there to give Kobe some deer meat and found a girl on their doorstep. Says she's Hailey's sister."

I've heard Hailey talk about her older sister and how much she misses her.

"Is she okay?" I ask.

There's silence from Lone Star. Then I hear a baby crying.

"Is that a baby?" asks Travis.

"Yup. She's got a baby with her."

Me and Travis share a look, and I know without asking to offer to help.

"Are they okay? Does she need somewhere to stay?"

"She's fine," he says. "I'll take care of it."

He hangs up the phone, and Travis and I shrug at each other.

"I guess she'll get back in her car and head home."

"I hope he's not offering his place."

Travis says it as a joke, and we both laugh at the thought of the reclusive, monosyllabic Lone Star who likes peace and quiet with a baby in his house.

We're distracted by my own baby moving in my belly. A smile lights up my face, and I take Travis's hand and place it over my belly. A moment later he feels the kick, and a broad grin spreads across his face.

"I can't wait to meet this little guy."

"Me too."

He leans forward and kisses my lips, and a warm feeling encases my heart. I've got my man and a baby on the way. It's everything my teenage self ever wanted.

* * *

WILD HOPE BONUS SCENE

TRAVIS

Three months later…

The toes are so tiny I can barely see them. His little feet wiggle, and his hands clasp thin air with palms so tiny that they're smaller than my thumb.

It's been three hours and thirteen minutes since we welcomed my son into the world. And I cannot stop staring at him.

He's perfect. Ten little fingers. Ten little toes. His eyes are squeezed shut, and his wrinkled little face is pointed towards my wife.

My amazing wife.

I'm still processing what I've witnessed over the last thirty-six hours of labor. I didn't know women were capable of such things. I mean, I knew it, but I didn't really know it until I saw it with my own eyes.

I've witnessed Kendra crouched over, making noises like a wounded animal. All I could do was mop the sweat off her brow and call the midwife, who assured me it was perfectly normal for my wife to be braying like a cow.

And then the pushing when I thought she'd rip in two and the glorious moment when my son slid out and into the waiting arms of the midwife. I cut the umbilical cord and laid him down on Kendra's chest and the little guy waggled his head, sniffing the air for her milk.

A nurse helped him latch for his first feed, and again I was filled with wonder. That my wife not only brought this new life into the world but is now feeding him, keeping him alive with her own body.

I've seen a lot of things in my time, but this has been the most humbling.

Now Kendra is sleeping and I've got Noah in my arms. I can't stop looking at the both of them, thinking about how lucky I am.

The curtain around the bed moves, and Quentin appears.

There's been tension between me and Quentin ever since Kendra and I got together. I thought it would ease once we were married, and it has on the surface. We're friends again, but I sense that he's holding back, that he still hasn't quite forgiven me for hooking up with his little sister.

Kendra wakes up, and she smiles at her brother.

Hey, Uncle."

He starts at his new moniker, and I hold the baby up to him.

Quentin stares at Noah and looks reluctant to take him. I don't blame him. Noah's so tiny he fits in the palm of my hand. It's not something we've been around before, babies.

"Meet Noah, your nephew."

Quentin takes him uncertainly and wraps his enormous hands around him. "Is he supposed to be that tiny?"

Kendra gives a tired smile. "Any bigger, and I would have had to have stitches. I'm lucky he's three weeks early."

The little guy was so keen to come out that he caught us all by surprise.

I watch Quentin carefully, because something's happening as he looks down at his nephew. The permanent frown he wears softens.

"Hey, little guy," he says. "Nice to meet you."

Noah reaches a tiny hand toward the sound of his voice and Quentin strokes the almost translucent fingers, a look of wonder spreading across his face.

"I'm your uncle."

Quentin's voice cracks, and he blinks quickly.

"Are you crying?" says Kendra incredulously.

Quentin wipes his eyes. "Nah, it's the dust from the road."

I share a look with Kendra and take her hand across the hospital bed. Quentin hands us back the baby.

"That's my nephew," he says proudly and slaps me on the back. His eyes are wet, and there's a genuine smile on his face.

"This is your family now, man. I know you'll take care of them." There must be more dust getting in his eyes, because he wipes them again. "Just going to use the washroom."

He exits hastily, but me and Kendra barely notice. Our eyes are on our son, our beautiful, perfect boy.

Maybe that dust is in the building, because as I look down at my beautiful wife cradling my son, there's a sting behind my eyes. She's radiant and exhausted, with a wide grin on her face as Noah latches onto her breast.

My heart opens, and I can't stop the tears of happiness at the sight of my family.

* * *

WILD RUNAWAY

WILD RUNAWAY

A single mom in danger and the ex-military biker who becomes her protector...

I found her on the doorstep with a baby in her arms.

A woman on the run, as damaged as I am.

We each have our demons from the past. Mine are internal and harder to fight, remnants from my days in the military. But I can take on Trish's demons.

When her ex comes to claim her, he doesn't expect to find an entire MC club of hardened ex-military mountain men fighting her corner.

Because I'll do anything to protect my wild runaway.

Wild Runaway is a single mom in danger, MC-lite romance featuring an ex-military protector hero and the curvy woman who runs away with his heart.

CONTENT ADVISORY

Dear Reader,

Joseph and Trish's story deals with issues of domestic abuse off the page. If you find this upsetting then please proceed with caution.

Rest assured, they get the HEA they deserve and Trish finds safety in the arms of her true protector hero.

-Sadie

1
JOSEPH

The half a deer carcass in the back of the pickup bumps up and down as I drive over the uneven surface of the mountain road. I watch it in the rearview mirror, wondering if I should have strapped it down better or if it'll jump right out of the crate.

It's a fresh kill from today, and I'm making good on my promise to give a shank to Kobe. He's got a baby on the way, and I don't mind sharing my meat with others on the mountain who need it.

The private gravel road that leads to Kobe and Hailey's cabin is lined with tall pine trees and scraggly bushes that scrape against the pickup as I turn in.

The driveway opens up to the front of their classic log cabin, and as I pull up out front, I note that Kobe's pickup isn't here. I guess I should have called ahead, but I like doing things the old-fashioned way. I grew up in the mountains, and if you wanted to visit your neighbor, and by neighbor I mean any other mountain dweller, you just turned up.

As I cut the engine, I realize there's someone sitting on the front steps.

A woman is hunched over on the stairs that lead down from the front porch. She's clutching something close to her chest, and her brown eyes are wide and staring. She's as frightened as a deer in the forest, and the way she's poised, with a hand on the banister and one foot on the bottom steps, ready to leap up at any moment, she's just as flighty.

We stare at each other, her breathing hard, clearly wondering if she should make a dash for it, and me paralyzed by the vision before me. Because she is a vision. Sunlight dances off her long golden hair as it cascades over her shoulders. She's got pale, smooth skin and full, youthful lips. Hell, she's at least ten years younger than me, but there's something in the set of her eyes, a wariness that makes her look older.

I don't know who she is or why she's here, but my instinct tells me any sudden movement could scare her off.

Instead of getting out of the car, I wind the window down and we stare at each other. My mouth goes dry as I drink her in. I've never seen anyone so beautiful, and I've got no clue what to say to her.

I clear my throat, and she startles. Christ, the woman's jumpier than a newborn fawn.

"Are you a friend of Hailey's?"

I take a guess that she's here for Kobe's wife. They look about the same age, and I figure if I drop Hailey's name she'll realize I'm not a stranger.

The woman pulls her eyebrows together and adjusts whatever it is she's clutching to her chest.

"Who are you?"

Her voice is bold, and I like that. She may be trembling like a deer, but she's putting on a show of bravado.

"Name's Joseph. I served with Kobe."

She relaxes a little. Being ex-military has that effect on people. They feel they can trust you because you served their country. But the things I saw people doing to each other over there made me lose all hope in humanity. It's why I live deep in the mountains, why I only come out for my motorcycle club or to run errands like this.

The rest of humanity can go to hell. I've seen too much madness. I've seen what people can do to each other, and I'd rather keep my own company with the animals of the forest.

If it weren't for the Wild Riders MC, I'd never leave my patch of forest at all. I hunt or grow most of the food I need and live off the grid with my own set-up. There's not much I need people for. But Kobe was a brother in arms, and we hunt together sometimes.

"Do you know where Kobe and Hailey are?" the woman asks without telling me her name.

She's afraid of something or someone, I'd bet my best gun on it. A wave of protectiveness hits me so suddenly that I sit back in my seat. I don't know this woman, but I want to keep her safe from whatever she's scared of. I just need her to trust me.

"Dunno. I stopped by to drop some meat off."

Her shoulders sag, and the thing she's holding to her chest moves. She glances down at it and readjusts herself. She's got something alive there, I'm sure. Maybe a puppy or something she found in the woods.

"You been waiting long?"

She stares at me long and hard, and I get the feeling she's assessing me. I tug on my beard, not sure how I measure up. A grizzled mountain man with half a deer in the back of his pickup. If I'd known I was going to meet this beauty today, I would have trimmed my beard and put my best flannel on.

Still, something must work in my favor, because she lets out a long breath and relaxes a little.

"I've been waiting for a few hours."

As she says it, a breeze rustles the surrounding trees, and whatever adrenaline she had warming her veins when I showed up dissipates, because she shivers and hunches over.

As she shivers, the bundle in her arms wriggles again and a thin cry pierces the air. Her attention snaps to the bundle and she bounces it up and down, making shushing noises.

Realization hits me.

"You've got a baby?"

She turns away and pulls the thing closer as if I'm

going to jump out and snatch it. My mind's working overtime wondering what the hell this young woman is doing sitting out in the cold with a baby for hours on end in nothing but a thin coat.

I glance around the area in case I've missed something, but there's no sign of a car. No indication of how she got here or what she's doing here. But she's cold and she's got a crying baby. She needs my help.

I open the cab to the pickup and she stands up and backs onto the deck, the flighty look coming into her eyes.

I hold my hands up.

"I'm not gonna hurt you. The wind's picking up and you look cold."

She bounces the baby and stares at me but doesn't respond. Tiny cries echo around the forest, and the sound is so alien to me it makes me wince. I turn away before she can see and get the blanket from the back.

I want to wrap it around her myself, take care of her so she can take care of her baby. But I sense any movement might scare her take off. And it's important to me that I keep talking to her.

I walk to the bottom of the stairs and hold the blanket up. She snatches it off me and retreats to the deck. Ignoring herself, she wraps it around the child, tucking it around the small body and leaving half of it trailing down her hip.

There's a small backpack leaning against the front door, but she doesn't appear to have anything else with her. I wonder again who she is and what she's doing here and why I feel so damn protective of her.

I can't leave her here on her own, especially with a baby.

"You want to call them and see if you can find out when they're coming home?"

She nods. "My phone's out of battery. I left in a hurry…" She snaps her mouth shut as if she's said too much.

I want to admonish her for venturing into the mountains on her own with only a light jacket and no means of communication. But she's obviously not from around here and doesn't know how dangerous the mountain can be. She probably doesn't even have bear spray.

I slide my phone out of my pocket.

"I don't have Hailey's number, but you can call Kobe."

I hold out the phone, and she takes it with her free arm. I'm rewarded with a small smile.

"Thank you."

I can hear the tone indicating that the call's not connecting. Wherever Kobe is he hasn't got signal, which isn't unusual. Parts of the mountain are blissfully still dark spots.

She hands back the phone, and her eyebrows are knit together with worry. The baby scrunches up its face and lets out a bellow.

"She's hungry."

There's a desperate tone to her voice, and I guess she hasn't got any food with her.

"I've got deer in the back if she wants some?"

It's meant to be a joke, even I know you don't feed raw meat to a baby, but the woman frowns. "She's not on solids yet. I've got milk in my bag but no way to heat it."

She sticks her chin out, daring me to call her a bad mother. Hell, I'm not judging. I don't know her circumstances, but I guess she wouldn't be out here in the cold with an infant if there wasn't a damn good reason for it.

"I can call some people and see if anyone knows where Kobe and Hailey are."

She tugs on her lower lip and looks away. She's worried about something. Maybe she doesn't want anyone to know she's here.

"I'll call Symon, the ranger. He knows the comings and goings of everyone on this mountain, and he's discreet."

She looks back at me and nods.

I bring up Symon's number as she jiggles the baby on her hip.

"Who will I say is looking for them?"

She bits her lip again, leaving imprints from her teeth. She worries it a lot, and I long to run my thumb over the puckered skin and smooth it out.

"Trish," she finally says. "I'm Hailey's sister."

"Trish." I like the sound of her name. It's fierce like she is. "I'll call the ranger."

I make the call to Symon, but no one picks up. I leave him a quick message without mentioning Trish.

Next, I call the Wild Taste Bar and Restaurant. It's

where the HQ for the Wild Riders MC is based. Kobe and Hailey often come over for lunch or a drink. Every man in the MC is ex-military, and Kobe knows a fair few of us. He's social for a mountain man and likes to keep in touch, but we all know he's checking in on us. Making sure no one falls over the edge of the precipice that so many of us came back tottering along.

Kendra picks up the phone. She's Barrel's sister and Hops's old lady. That caused a huge stir and nearly got Hops banished from the club, but luckily they sorted out their differences.

"Are Kobe and Hailey up there?"

Kendra checks the restaurant, but no one's seen them. Hops is speaking in the background, and Kendra must hand the phone across to him.

"They're away for the weekend. Went to the coast."

That will explain the phone. They've probably got a remote spot where there's no signal. Having some time together before the baby arrives.

"I went up there to give Kobe some deer meat and found a girl on their doorstep. Says she's Hailey's sister."

Trish gives me a worried look, but I can trust my MC brothers. They won't breathe a word.

"Is she okay?" Kendra asks.

I glance at Trish, and she's cradling the baby. The shushing seems to have worked, but all of a sudden the infant lifts its tiny pink head and gives an almighty wail.

"Is that a baby?" asks Hops.

The pink mouth is contorted into an angry cry that's so loud it's scaring the birds away.

"Yup, she's got a baby with her."

Trish bounces the infant on her shoulder as she paces the porch. Tiny fingers grasp at her hair, and she looks down at the pink scrunched up face with love. Even though the thing is screaming at her, even though it's cold and windy and I just felt the first drops of rain, all I see emanating from her is love.

A bolt of realization shoots through my veins. I want that love trained on me.

The thought is so strong it makes me stagger. I don't know anything about this curvy beauty, but she's vulnerable out here. Her and the baby, they need me. My heart does a little flip, and my chest swells with new purpose.

Whatever this woman is running from, whatever she and her baby need, I will provide. A surge of protectiveness rushes through me, and I know I'll do whatever it takes to keep Trish and her baby safe.

Kendra's saying something on the other end of the line, asking if they need help, but I barely hear her. I know my purpose; I know what I need to do.

"She's fine," I say. "I'll take care of it."

I hang up the phone and slide it back in my pocket. I've never been around a baby, and it's been years since I was with a woman. But I'll do whatever I need to do to take care of these two.

2
TRISH

I keep my face turned down, focusing on the tiny bundle in my arms. It's been over five hours since Rose had her last bottle. The train took me to the town of Hope, and I stopped at a cafe where they let me heat up a bottle for her even though I didn't buy anything.

My tummy rumbled at the cakes and sticky pastries in the cabinet, but I couldn't risk spending any money unnecessarily.

When I left home this morning, I only had time to grab the backpack I kept stashed in the bottom of Rose's diaper drawer, the one place Ian would never go.

The cafe let me use their phone to call Hailey, but it didn't connect. I found the only taxi in town and used the last of my money to take it up the mountain. My cash didn't quite cover the fair and I said I'd walk the rest of the way, but the kind man insisted on driving me all the way.

When I took the cash from what Ian thinks is his secret stash this morning, I thought there would be more, but it barely covered the cost of getting here. I'm at the mercy of my sister and strangers, and that terrifies me.

I couldn't choose the time of my leaving, so it wasn't a surprise that Hailey and Kobe weren't in. But it was five hours waiting on their doorstep until the giant man in the mud-splattered pickup turned up.

I watch Joseph out of the corner of my eye as he speaks on the phone. He's the biggest man I've ever seen, even bigger than my brother-in-law, Kobe. Joseph has a full rugged beard and the brightest blue eyes I've ever seen. They seem out of place in his weathered, tanned face. Too bright and blue for a mountain man.

He ends the call and slides the phone into his pocket.

"They've gone away for a few days."

The words make my heart sink and I sag to the ground, feeling the weight of what I've done.

Hailey was my last chance, the only place I could turn. I never expected she wouldn't be here when I turned up. But I can't go back, and not just because I don't have the funds. I'd rather camp out in the woods than go back to Ian.

Tears threaten my eyes and I blink them back quickly, but not before Joseph sees.

"Hey." His voice is a gentle rumble and soothes a deep

part of my soul. "You can shelter at my place until they get back."

I jerk my head up. He seems nice and he's been kind, but I just met this stranger.

"We're fine."

He keeps his eyes on me, not convinced.

"You don't know me, Trish, but you need shelter and that baby needs milk. You can heat the bottle in my kitchen and do what you need to do to look after that baby, and I'll stay out in the pickup if that makes you feel better."

It does. Kind of. But also a little disappointed. I might not know this mountain giant, but the way he looks at me makes my body come alive in a way I haven't felt in a long time. I push the thought away. I have to do what's best for my daughter.

A gust of wind whips my hair around my face, and a drop of rain hits my cheek. I look up at the darkening sky. Rose howls, and I snap my gaze back to her. The way her face puckers with hunger makes my heart hurt. Whatever I do, I need to do something soon.

"I don't have much choice."

Joseph stares at me. "You do have a choice," he says slowly. "I can drive you somewhere, anywhere you want to go, or back to wherever you came from."

I shudder, and he notices.

"Or to a hotel if you prefer."

I lower my eyes, not wanting him to see the shame

that heats my face. I don't have any money. I'm completely reliant on the kindness of this stranger.

I look at Joseph long and hard, mentally running through the things I know about him. He's a friend of Kobe's, and Kobe doesn't suffer fools, so he must be a decent guy. He's ex-military, but for the first time I notice what he's wearing over his faded flannel shirt: a motorcycle club jacket with a patch.

"You're in an MC?"

My danger sense goes up a notch, and I pull Rose close.

"The Wild Riders. We're ex-military guys who love to ride. That's all. No funny business, no hassle."

Where I come from, an MC means bad news. They ride around on their big bikes intimidating the locals and getting in trouble with the law. But again, what choice do I have?

"Okay," I say, hoping like hell I don't regret it.

I go to grab my bag from the porch, but he gets there first. As I straighten up our arms brush, and a spark of heat jumps from his body to mine. I gasp, and my eyes meet his. From this close up, I see all the shades of blue in their depths. There are lines around his eyes, a weariness that tells of hurt.

Joseph may be kind and genuine, but there's pain in his past too. I'm sure of it. For some strange reason I find that comforting, seeing my pain reflected in him.

Then he smiles and his eyes sparkle, and the moment passes.

He takes my bag and opens the pickup's back door. "Come on. Let's get your baby some milk."

3
JOSEPH

My gaze slides to the rearview mirror and Trish sitting in the backseat.

Blonde hair falls over her face as she gazes down at her baby. The motion of the pickup seems to have lulled it to sleep, and a smile spreads over Trish's lips as she watches her daughter.

There's something warming in the way she's looking at the baby that I can't look away from. She's the picture of motherhood, despite the dark shadows under her eyes and unwashed hair. Her expression is serene when she watches her daughter.

Trish must feel my gaze on her, because she glances up and our eyes meet. I look away quickly, but not before I see the haunted expression in her eyes. She may appear serene when she watches her daughter, but there's a restless energy about her at other times. She's running from something, but I don't know what.

I take the drive easy, aware of my precious cargo in the back seat. Trish's nose twitched when she got in next to the deer, but she had the good grace not to say anything about her bloody companion.

There's not a lot I can do about the deer carcass riding alongside her. I don't know how long Kobe will be away, so I didn't want to leave it. I'll stick it in the deep freeze and give it to them when they get back.

We arrive at my cabin as the sky is turning grey with dusk. Trish bites her lip when she sees my ramshackle cabin in the woods. It's not a nicely constructed cabin like Kobe's. My cabin was put together with my own two hands. I felled the trees, cleared the small area of land, and built it myself while living in a temporary shelter nearby.

Solar panels cover the roof, catching the rays that come through the clearing, and water comes from a well I dug in the ground.

It's one bedroom, all this single man has needed, until now.

By the time we get out of the car, the baby's crying again. This time it's angry cries, and even I can tell the poor little thing is hungry.

"What do you need?" I ask Trish as soon as we get inside. I dump her bag in the entryway and switch on the lights for the kitchen.

The cabin is an open plan with the kitchen on the right and the living room on the left. A small table sits against the wall and there are two steps that lead to the bedroom and the bathroom.

"Hot water to heat the bottle or a microwave if you have it."

I'm not big on appliances, so I get the kettle boiling for the water. Trish crouches next to her bag and attempts to open it with one hand while cradling the baby. I haven't seen her put the thing down, and I wonder if she ever does.

"Let me help."

I crouch down to open the bag for her, but instead she holds the baby toward me. Its tiny mouth is wide open, and the noise emanating from it makes my ears bleed.

Trish gives me a reassuring smile. "Can you take her while I fix the bottle? It'll be quicker."

I'm touched that she trusts me enough to hold the infant, but I'm not sure she should. I've never held a baby before. I'm more used to wielding axes and hunting rifles, not tiny babies who wiggle and cry.

"You'll be fine. Just hold her like you would a football."

I take the infant uncertainly, and I must look terrified because Trish laughs. For a moment, the haunted expression leaves her eyes and they sparkle like sun reflecting on a mountain lake. Then she turns her attention to getting the things she needs from her bag.

I hold the baby in front of me, not sure what to do. She's

staring at her momma and wiggling like a hare caught in a trap. There's an acrid stench coming from under the blanket that must mean she needs a diaper change.

I glance at Trish, but she's busy in the kitchen mixing formula into a bottle. I'm on my own.

"Hey," I say to the baby.

She looks startled by my voice and her head turns to look at me, the crying stopping for a moment.

Warmth spreads in my chest. I made the baby stop crying. We stare at each other, her curious blue eyes looking at me expectantly. I don't know what to do. I'm not much of a talker at the best of times, and I know fuck all about talking to a baby.

When I don't say anything, her eyes scrunch up and her mouth opens.

"Hey," I say quickly. I guess my voice is lower and gruffer than what she's used to, because she stares at me again.

Her little hand reaches out and grabs my beard. She looks surprised at the texture, and her brow furrows in an adorable frown.

I don't know what to say to a baby, so I smile and introduce myself.

"I'm Joseph. Some people call me Lone Star."

Her face squeezes up, and just when I think I'm winning her over, she lets out a howl that would scare the bears from the woods.

Trish comes over and takes her off me, and it's a relief

to hand her over. I can coax a wild deer out of a trap, but I've got no idea how to calm a human baby.

"Let's get you changed while your milk's warming."

She looks around the cabin, and I wonder how it looks through the eyes of a mom. There's an open fireplace with a deerskin rug on the wooden floor and a sharp-edged coffee table. On one wall is my gun rack, and on the other are floor to ceiling windows, clear glass that looks straight into the depths of the dark forest.

Nope, it's not designed for babies, and I have a pang of regret. When I built this place, it was with myself in mind. Now I wonder what it would be like to have Trish and the baby around for good.

I shake the thought out of my head. It would be noisy and stinky if the last few minutes are anything to go by.

"Is there somewhere I can change her?"

I stare at her blankly until I realize she's talking about changing the diaper.

"The bedroom? Or the floor or the kitchen table?"

I don't know what she needs. I've never had a baby in my cabin before.

"Any flat surface will do." She slings her bag over her shoulder. "But probably not the kitchen table." Her nose crinkles up in an adorable way, and she smiles.

"You can use the bed."

She throws her bag over her shoulder and follows me into the bedroom. "I don't have a changing mat. Do you have an old towel or something I can throw down, just in case?"

I don't want to know what the just in case is. I grab a towel from the hallway closet and put it on my bed.

Trish lays the baby down, and I avert my eyes before I see something that can't be unseen.

"The bathroom's through there." I indicate the closed door as I shuffle out of the room, trying not to see the unwrapping of the diaper. "There's a bath if you want to bathe her. Or yourself."

An image of Trish naked and in my bath fills my head, and I practically run out of the bedroom. This woman's got me thinking about things I thought I was done with in my life.

I grip the kitchen counter and breathe hard, trying to control the storm of emotions inside me. How can one woman and one tiny baby make me feel so out of control?

"Get it together," I mutter to myself. She needs shelter, not a man ogling her and imagining her naked.

There's a stack of wood by the fire, and I get the fire going to warm the place up.

Trish comes out a few moments later and tests the milk, then settles with the baby on the couch to feed.

With a dry diaper and milk in her belly, the crying finally stops. A content silence settles on the cabin. It's a lovely sight, Trish feeding the baby in front of the fire, the only sounds the crackle of the flames and the baby suckling.

The silence is golden, and I release a breath I didn't know I was holding.

"Do they always cry that much?"

Trish glances up. "It's been a long day. Her routine is out of whack."

I want to ask why her day has been long and what she's running from. But at that moment the baby stirs, and Trish's attention is back on her daughter.

I leave her to it while I get busy in the kitchen. Trish looks like she needs looking after just as much as the baby. And I'll be the one to take care of her.

4
TRISH

With Rose's needs met, my anxiety eases a little. My baby girl is fed and changed, and we have shelter and a safe place to stay. It's more than we've had since she was born four months ago.

I've only known Joseph for a few short hours, but I'm starting to relax around him. A man who helps a woman and baby in need can't be all bad.

I wish I could get hold of Hailey, but hers and Kobe's phones are still out of range of any signal. With Rose fed, I realize how woefully unprepared I am. There's nowhere for her to sleep.

Joseph offers up his bed, which is so kind of him that I almost cry. But I turn away quickly and help him roll up towels to form a barrier for Rose. It's not ideal and I probably won't sleep a wink, but it will have to do until I can figure out my next move.

Joseph leaves me alone to get Rose down to sleep,

and I lie on the bed with her and hold her close. The bed smells masculine, like pine and oil, and a new sensation weaves itself into my veins. What would it be like to lie in here with Joseph, to have his muscular arms wrapped around me, to feel his body pressed against mine?

I shake the thought out of my head. There's no point having indecent thoughts about my rescuer. He's just a kind man doing the decent thing.

Rose makes a contented gurgling sound, and I kiss the top of her downy head.

"I'm sorry this was a bad day, baby girl." My hand rubs circles on her back as she snuggles into my chest. "But I hope it will be worth it."

There's a knot in my stomach that has been there since this morning, but as I press Rose's tiny body close and breathe in her milky scent, the knot eases a little.

My daughter is safe, and that's all that matters. Hailey will be home soon, and then I'll figure something out for us.

Hailey always told me I could come to her anytime. That's what sisters are for. She tried to get me to leave Ian sooner, but I stupidly thought things would get better once we had the baby. They didn't. They got worse.

Rose's breathing turns heavy, and I watch her sleep for a few minutes before placing her carefully between the towels and tiptoeing out of the bedroom.

The scent of frying garlic and rosemary hits me, and my stomach gives a lurching rumble. I cross my arms over it, horrified that Joseph heard. But he doesn't say anything.

"I've made stew."

He indicates for me to sit at the small kitchen table, and I slump into the seat. With Rose asleep, the adrenaline I've been running on all day leaves my body and I'm suddenly exhausted.

Joseph puts a large bowl of stew in front of me, and I attack it hungrily.

"Thank you," I say between mouthfuls.

I don't know what the meat is, but it's rich and lean, and with all the flavors he's included it's the best meal I've ever had.

"I'll pay you back for all this." Although I'm not sure how.

He shakes his head. "No you won't."

I choke on my mouthful, wondering if he can tell I don't have a dime to my name.

"You and the little one can stay as long as you need. Don't worry about money or any kind of payback."

He says it in a tone as if it's all decided. Like taking a stranger and her baby in are normal things to do. And maybe they are if you're a good person.

Suddenly, there's a sting of tears behind my eyes. The one person who was supposed to love me treated me like shit, yet this stranger has taken me and my child in, fed us, and given us shelter. I didn't know there was still this level of kindness in the world.

"Hell, don't cry."

Joseph reaches across the table and lays his meaty hand over mine. The warmth from him makes me sob harder.

"Sorry," I say between tears. "You've been so kind."

With his warm hand on mine, the first kind touch I've had in months, the flood gates open and I can't stop them. Everything I've been holding back for the last few months bubbles up inside me.

Joseph doesn't ask questions, which is good because I'm not ready to tell my story. Instead, he comes around to my side of the table and crouches next to my chair. His strong arms fold around me and he holds me silently as I cry, snot running into his checkered shirt.

We stay like that for a long time until my sobs dry up. I feel utterly drained when I sit back on my chair. But the knot in my stomach has lessened, and my chest feels less tight. For the first time today, I feel like I did the right thing.

Joseph trains his sparkling blue eyes on me. They're full of concern and warmth and a flash of something else. I recognize it as desire before he sits back on his haunches and looks down.

My body tingles. I'm red-eyed and puffy and covered in snot, but one look from this man has my core clenching and heat coursing through my veins.

It's been a long time since someone held me and a long time since a man looked at me with desire, no matter how fleeting. I need to get a grip.

"Thank you, Joseph. I mean it. We had nowhere else to go today."

He lifts his hand, and I think he's going to touch my face, but instead he does this awkward pat on my head.

"I'll look after you, Trish. You and the baby. You have nothing to worry about again."

His words are confusing. The tone sounds final, like he'll always look after me and Rose, but that's ridiculous. He must just mean while we're here.

He stands back on his feet and clears the bowls away.

I try to help with the washing up, but Joseph won't let me. Instead, he runs a bath for me and insists I bathe and get to sleep. I don't fight it; the day has left me exhausted, and I can barely keep my eyes open.

"I'll sleep in the pickup so you have nothing to worry about," he says.

I shake my head. "You don't need to do that. It's bad enough that we've taken your bed. At least sleep on the couch."

I barely know him, but I feel I can trust Joseph. More than that, as I soak in his giant bathtub, my thoughts go to the feel of his arms around me, how he smelled like pine and rosemary, the way my heartbeat quickened when he hugged me, and those sparkling blue intense eyes.

I shake the thoughts out of my head. He's the first man who's been kind. That's all it is. He'd do the same for anyone, and if there's one lesson I should have learned by now, it's not to get carried away when a man shows you kindness. It doesn't last.

But he's different.

My heart whispers things to me that I'm not ready to hear.

I drain the bath and snuggle next to Rose. She seems safe enough in her makeshift towel crib, and I'm soon fast asleep.

5

JOSEPH

Mornings are my favorite time in the cabin. With a steaming coffee, I sit out on the porch listening to the bird chatter, the wind rustling the leaves, and the wildlife shuffling through the undergrowth.

But the morning after Trish and the baby crash into my world is different.

It's before dawn when the cries reach my ears. They're muffled, coming from the bedroom, but they permeate the stillness of the cabin.

I pad to the bedroom door and hear Trish making shushing noises. The baby's probably hungry and needs a bottle.

I knock gently and push the door open, intending to let Trish know I'm awake and she can use the kitchen to heat the bottle. But the words die on my lips.

She's wearing one of my t-shirts, which hangs almost

to her knees and hugs her curvy figure. One side is snagged on Rose's blanket and it pulls upward, exposing a thick creamy thigh. My mouth goes dry as I think about sliding my hand up the t-shirt and discovering what's at the top of her luscious thighs. I drag my gaze away, but my dirty thoughts follow as I glimpse her tits pushed up against the t-shirt. She's braless, and the shape of her nipple presses against the cotton.

My dick stirs to life, and I've barely got my eyes open but I'm already imagining all sorts of dirty things I want to do to her.

I turn away, intending to get out of here before Trish sees the tenting in my track pants. She's pacing the room jiggling Rose on her hip, but before I can retreat, she sees me.

"Sorry we woke you."

I shake my head. "Don't matter." I'm an early riser anyway. "She need milk?"

Trish nods and follows me to the kitchen. I focus on what she and the baby need, trying to calm my racing male blood. I thought I was done with women, but twelve hours with this one in my cabin and my body's behaving like I'm a teenager.

Trish holds Rose while I get the formula ready, trying to remember what I saw her do yesterday. The tin of formula is light when I pick it up, and I have to tip it sideways to get to the powder at the bottom. I don't know if she's got any more in her bag, but this won't last another day.

While the bottle warms, Trish changes Rose and I make the coffee. Then we all sit out on the porch, the baby wrapped in a blanket as she sucks on her bottle.

As soon as Rose gets the teat of the bottle in her mouth, the crying finally stops. The silence is golden and we sit without talking, listening to the birdsong and the sound of the forest waking up.

"It's peaceful out here." Trish lets out a long sigh.

I take a sip of coffee and lean back in my chair.

"Yup."

The porch is positioned to face a clearing where the sun rises every morning. The pale rays warm my face and I close my eyes, enjoying the sounds of the baby suckling as Trish rocks her chair back and forth. I got the rocking chairs because I like the motion, but they're perfect for nursing babies.

A vision springs into my head, Trish and the baby here every morning by my side, rocking gently on the porch as we watch the sunrise.

A smile creeps over my face. I've never contemplated being with anyone until now, let alone a woman and a baby. But I like having Trish and Rose here. It's soothing to watch her with the baby in a way that speaks to my damaged soul.

When I came back from the military, I didn't want to be around people. I'd seen the worst of humanity, but Trish is showing me the best. The love of a mother and the fierce protectiveness toward her young.

I didn't have any family when I got out of the military

and Kobe told me about the Wild Riders MC, a motorcycle club of ex-servicemen. I've always loved to ride and I grew up in the mountains of the west, but there was nothing left for me back home. So I came here to see what it was about.

I like my quiet secluded life in the forest, but once a week I head down the mountain for the MC meetings and take part in any charity runs they're doing. I've helped my brothers build their own cabins, and I supply meat to the restaurant and to anyone who needs it.

Out here, I don't need much. I live off the land and off my military pension. I hunt and trap and sell meat and hides to the surrounding towns.

It's a good life. It's a single man's life. But now, for the first time, I want to share it with someone else. The thought both pleases and terrifies me. I'm an old man compared to Trish. I'm thirty-six, old and damaged. I have nightmares, haunted by what I saw humans do to each other. I don't like loud noises or being around people.

I stand up abruptly, not wanting to think about my failings. The best I can do is make Trish and the baby comfortable.

"I'm going for a supply run in town. What do you need?"

She hesitates, and I'm not sure if it's because of a reluctance to ask for help or if she doesn't have any money.

"I'll put it on my store account, so you don't have to pay me yet."

She doesn't have to pay me ever, but she's too proud to take charity. I've seen that before with people who need help.

"Umm." She bites her lower lip, and I wonder what's got her so troubled. I wish I could take her troubles away and make her smile and laugh like a young woman should.

"I need diapers and formula."

She looks away, and I'm sure there's more she needs, but I don't want to embarrass her. I'll pick up some baby stuff and hope it's right.

"Help yourself to anything in the cabin."

I figure getting out of the way and giving her time to get used to the place will help her relax. I head down the porch and turn around at the bottom step.

"And if you go walking in the forest, take some bear spray."

Her mouth pops open, and she pulls Rose to her chest as her eyes dart to the forest.

"Stick near the cabin and you'll be fine."

She doesn't look reassured, and I make a mental note to give her a lesson on basic mountain safety when I get back.

I chuckle to myself as I get into the pickup. This small town girl doesn't know a thing about the mountains, and I can't wait to teach her.

. . .

A few hours later, I'm at the general store in Wild. It's easy enough to get diapers here and formula, but I'll have to go across the mountain to Hope to get the other things I need.

Larry, who runs the store, looks at me suspiciously when I put the diapers down on the counter. But I don't say anything. It's none of his damn business, and I don't want to let the whole town know about Trish.

There's a baby store in Hope, and I browse the aisles trying to figure out what Rose needs. There are all in one outfits and cute animal t-shirts and tiny little dresses. I forgot to ask how old Rose is, but if human babies don't wean until six months, she must be younger than that. I pick up a cute onesie with a smiling giraffe and another with a fox. I stay away from the laughing bear; I don't want her to think bears are approachable.

Geez, if any of the guys were here they'd give me shit. But I already feel like a protective dad towards this baby.

There are a bunch of baby toys and I rifle through them, trying to find one that isn't a choking hazard. I settle on a colorful caterpillar and a wind-up car that will work well on my wooden floors.

I'm guessing Trish doesn't have a lot of baby clothes in that little bag of hers, so I throw in a couple of singlets and a baby changing mat. I find a travel crib and a baby sling. I've noticed Rose doesn't like to be put down, and this way she can stay close to her momma while Trish keeps her hands free.

I take it all to the counter and scowl when I recognize

Trudy. The last time I saw Trudy was when I helped install a ramp at their house after her son had an injury and needed assistance. She'd spent the entire time telling me and the boys all the gossip on the mountain, as if we care who's seeing who and who's newly divorced and whose daughter is off to college.

"Hello Joseph." She eyes the baby stuff I put on the counter. "You got some news you want to tell me?"

Her eyes light up, eager for the gossip.

The last thing I want to do is get into a conversation about Trish. Trudy's a decent woman, but I know how town gossip works. It spreads quicker than wildfire around these mountains.

"Got a friend staying for a few days."

She wants to ask more, but I cut her off with a question about washing instructions on the baby clothes.

While she's talking, I pay up and get out of there as soon as she hands me my bags. Her curious look follows me out of the shop.

I'm walking back to the pickup when a glint of bronze in a shop window catches my eye. I stop in front of a boutique jewelry shop and stare at the clip in the window display. Trish's hair always slips over her shoulder, and a clip would help her keep it out of the way. And she'd look damn good with her hair half clipped back.

I stop into the shop, smiling to myself as I imagine her face when I give it to her.

6

TRISH

With the peace and quiet of the cabin, the knot in my stomach unwinds as the morning goes on. I give Rose tummy time on the rug, and she giggles as I pull funny faces at her.

We go for a walk outside but not too far from the cabin. Joseph freaked me out when he talked about bears.

There's a vegetable garden surrounded by chicken wire and a greenhouse with the last of the season's tomatoes. I pull out a few weeds and pick a shiny red tomato to have with lunch.

Rose gets restless, so I bring her in for another bottle and change her into the last diaper. It reminds me how lucky we are to have found Joseph. If he hadn't have shown up at Hailey's, I don't know what I would have done. And if I didn't have Hailey to run to in the first place…

I shudder at the thought and pull Rose close to my chest.

She gurgles happily, and I walk her around the cabin until she falls asleep. It's usually the only way she can get to sleep, resting on me. Maybe she tuned in to the turmoil that was going on in the trailer where we came from. But for whatever reason, she won't sleep unless she's pressed up against me.

I walk around the cabin, rhythmically pacing until her breathing gets heavy. Once I know she's asleep, I slow down and peer at the photos on the cabin walls.

There's a group of men in front of big motorbikes like the one I noticed parked in a shed behind the cabin. They're all wearing the same leather jackets that Joseph has, but for a motorcycle club, they look friendlier than I would have imagined. I find Joseph near the back. He's the only one not smiling. His blue eyes stare intently at the camera.

Another photo shows him in his military uniform, standing tall with a group of men. He looks haunted, his gaze looking down, unable to meet the eye of the camera.

It makes me wonder why he left the military and how he ended up here. There's a lot I don't know about Joseph, only that he's kind and I feel safe in his presence. And for now, that's enough.

My arm aches, and I risk putting Rose down. I ease her between the towels of the makeshift baby bed, holding my breath as I lower her onto the bedding. She stirs but doesn't wake up. Relieved, I tip-toe out of the room but leave the door open so I'll hear her as soon as she wakes.

I make myself another cup of coffee and a tomato and cheese sandwich and eat them with my feet tucked under me on the couch. I try Hailey again, but the call doesn't connect. If she was going away on a big vacation, she would have told me, so it's likely this trip is only a weekend break and she'll be back tomorrow.

Then what?

When I left the trailer, I didn't have a plan past getting the hell away from Ian. I knew my sister would take me in, and I could figure out my next move from there. It's hard to make plans when you're fighting for survival.

I guess I'll look for a job and a place to stay. Hailey's got her own baby on the way, so I don't want to intrude on them for any longer than I have to.

If only I could stay here forever. It's so peaceful and Joseph is so kind, not to mention the way my core tightens whenever he's nearby.

I'm pulled out of my thoughts by the sound of a car. My gut clenches, and I duck behind the couch with my heart racing. My hands grip the top of the couch, and I'm about to make a dash to the bedroom to get Rose when I recognize Joseph's pickup.

It's just Joseph returning.

Of course it is. You're safe here.

I get out from behind the couch before he can see me. My heart's still racing, and I check on Rose. The sight of her sleeping peacefully calms my nerves.

I pull the door almost shut so we don't wake her, then head outside to help Joseph with the shopping.

"I'll give you a hand."

He grunts and nods, which I'm learning means thank you. He's a man of few words, and I like that. I'm also learning that he might not talk much, but he thinks a lot. Behind his quiet demeanor, his brain is working overtime.

I grab a shopping bag from the back and gasp in surprise when I see the name on the bag.

"You went to Babyland?" It's a franchise of baby gear that's way out of my price range.

"Noticed you need a few things."

By a few things, he means two big shopping bags worth. My heart warms at his thoughtfulness. I've never felt so cared for, and I still can't believe it's a complete stranger that's looking after me and Rose.

In the bags are baby clothes, toys, a changing mat, and a sling, which will save my sore arm. Joseph must have noticed how I'm always carrying her around, how she cries whenever I put her down. The thoughtfulness makes my eyes sting and I blink quickly, not wanting to cry again.

"This will have to do for now, until I can build you a proper one."

Joseph holds a box that says 'travel crib' on the side. It must have cost a fortune.

"You didn't have to do this." My eyes are welling up, and damn this man who makes me cry and makes my body tingle and makes me feel safe and normal for the first time in months.

"You're mine to look after Trish, you and Rose."

His words are confusing again, because Rose is not his baby and her biological father isn't interested in caring for her, so why would this stranger be? But I like the idea of being his.

"Here." He hands me a small package. "This one's for you."

I open the brown wrapping paper and turn the object over in my hand.

It's a hair comb, a polished bronze design with a cluster of pink roses on the side. It's beautiful and not what I was expecting from a man like Joseph.

"So you can keep your hair pinned back. It gets in the way when you're feeding the little one."

Tears sting my eyes. It's the most thoughtful gift anyone's ever given me, and it's from a virtual stranger.

"Thank you." But I can't say anything else or I'll cry again.

Joseph must sense that, because he takes the clip off me. "May I?"

I love that he asked before he touched me, because I probably would have flinched if he hadn't. His rough hand slides over my silky hair, and the sensation sends sparks of heat through my body. He's so close his woodsy scent tickles my nostrils and make me want to pull him closer.

I close my eyes and inhale, loving the way he smells of

fresh pine and woodsmoke, loving his touch and letting the sensations unfurling in my belly warm me up.

This is what it feels like to be touched by a man. Gentle, loving, and with care. Not rough and mean and hurtful.

I feel Joseph's touch all the way through my body to my very soul. Warmth spreads though my veins, warming up my belly and snaking right to my core. Heat wells up between my legs, and my core throbs with need.

It's been so long since I was touched with tenderness, and a whimper escapes my lips as Joseph scoops my hair off my neck and slides the clip into place.

He's so close that his breath tickles my skin, sending tendrils of heat through my veins. His fingers pause behind my ear, and his breathing is ragged. Neither of us move and I hold my breath, not wanting this moment to end.

His fingertips brush behind my ear and trail down the soft skin of my neck. I tilt my head back, an invitation to keep going, hardly daring to breathe. He leans forward and gently presses his mouth to the delicate skin at the nape of my neck. At his touch, my body is on fire. I whimper as his mouth moves over my skin, his fingers sliding under the collar of my t-shirt.

Suddenly, he stiffens. And I freeze, remembering what's caused him to stop. I pull away, but it's too late.

"Who did this to you?"

His voice has a dangerous edge that I've not heard from him before, and it sets warning bells ringing. I scoot to the other side of the room, putting myself between him and Rose.

He must see the fear in my eyes, because his voice softens.

"I'm not going to hurt you, Trish. I would never hurt you. But somebody has."

You get so used to living with the marks on your body that you forget they're there. The fingerprints on my neck, the bruising on my collar. I run my hand over them now, embarrassed that Joseph has seen them.

"Is that why you ran?"

Joseph has his hands up in a placating gesture and he's trying to keep his voice calm, but there's rage simmering underneath.

"Yes," I whisper.

The confession feels good. I've never admitted it to anyone before. I couldn't tell Hailey, because I was too ashamed. She wouldn't have understood how you could stay with a man who does that to you.

"Do you want to tell me about it?"

I hesitate. I've never talked about the way Ian treated me. It's embarrassing to admit that the person who's supposed to love you hurts you.

But as I look at Joseph, this burly man who could snap me in two if he wanted but has shown me nothing but kindness, I feel exhausted.

I'm tired of hiding. I'm tired of pretending everything's okay. I want to tell him; I want him to see all my hidden parts. I feel I can trust him with my hurt.

Joseph takes a seat on the couch, and I join him. And once I start talking, I can't stop.

I tell him about Ian being my high school boyfriend and how it started out well, but when we moved into the trailer together things changed.

How I was going to leave him, but then I got pregnant. I thought the baby would change things, but it made them worse. He couldn't cope with the crying. He blamed me and took it out on me. That I could handle.

But the morning I left, he squeezed my neck so hard that I passed out. When I came to, he was standing over the crib with Rose in his hands. She was screaming as he held her in front of him. I grabbed her off him before he could do anything. I don't know if he would have hurt her, but I wasn't going to stick around to find out.

Ian left the trailer and I grabbed our bag, took the jar of money he had stashed away, and fled.

That's why I have hardly anything with us. I couldn't risk staying another moment in that place. I had to get her away from him.

Joseph listens in silence. A vein pulsing on his neck is the only indication that he's taking it all in and how angry it's making him to hear.

After I finish telling him my pathetic story, he takes my hand in his, his blue eyes sparking dangerously.

"I'll kill that fucking asshole."

There's a grim conviction in his voice that makes me shiver. I'm reminded of the man in uniform, the military man, the trained killer. I hate Ian, but I'd never want anyone dead.

"Don't do that," I whisper. "I got away from him. I'm never going back."

Joseph pulls me toward him, and I sink into his warmth. His touch is electric, and I want him to keep kissing me the way he was before he saw the marks on my neck.

"I promise you this, Trish. I will never let anything happen to you or Rose. You understand?"

I nod, although I'm not sure I do. How can this virtual stranger make this promise to me and the daughter that isn't his? But I can tell by the conviction in his voice that he's serious.

"You're mine to protect. And I will protect you both with my life."

It's a pledge, and a man who's sworn an oath to die for his country doesn't make promises lightly. The tightness in my stomach eases, and I lean into him.

I've got Joseph fighting in my corner. I don't understand why, but it feels right.

7
JOSEPH

*P*rez bangs the gavel on the table, and the chatter in the room dies down.

Twelve sets of eyes turn to face him, ready for our weekly meeting. We're sitting around the thick pine table, felled and carved from a tree in the local forest. The club meeting room is out the back of the Wild Taste Restaurant and overlooks the courtyard where the brewery and mechanic shop are. The colorful flags hanging outside Danni's gallery brighten the place up. She opened it a few months ago, and it's a hit with the tourists. Danni is Colter's old lady, and the entire club got behind the venture.

"First order of business. We've been asked to help Angie with renovations to her bar."

Angie lives on the other side of the mountain and runs a restaurant and bar the same as we do. Her husband died in active service a few years ago leaving her with two kids. It was a hell of a sacrifice and we've helped her out over the years, when she lets us.

"Isn't her husband's best friend sniffing dating her now?" says Barrels.

He eyes Hops as he says it, still not comfortable with the fact that his best friend is with his sister. There are murmurs around the table and angry mutterings.

I swear this place is like a gossip house some days, grown men giving their opinion on whether a woman should stay true to her husband after he passed in the line of service. It's an uncomfortable thought, but it's been seven years. You can't expect her to stay celibate for the rest of her life.

After some discussion, we vote unanimously to help Angie. It doesn't matter what her current circumstances are. She lost her husband to this country and spent the last seven years raising their children on her own. She deserves all the help she can get.

Marcus offers to supply any timber she needs from his family sawmill, while we all pledge to help with whatever labor she needs.

There are a few other points of business, info about a charity run we're doing in a few weeks, and then Specs goes over the accounts.

Maggie brings in a plate of pastries from the kitchen and scurries back out as quickly as she can. Our shy pastry chef is one hell of a cook but timid as heck. I notice Arlo's gaze following her out of the room.

It's when Prez asks if there's any more business that I clear my throat.

All eyes turn to me. I haven't said anything in the meeting which isn't unusual. I'm an observer and keep my opinions to myself unless asked. But this is something I need the entire club to help with.

"There's a woman staying with me."

The Prez's eyebrows shoot up his head, and some of the other guys look surprised. The fuckers. They probably think I kidnapped her or something.

"She's fleeing a bad situation, her and her baby."

My fists clench when I think about what Trish told me yesterday. How anyone can hurt a woman is beyond me, and I stayed up all night thinking about it. I promised I wouldn't go after the fucker, but I'll do all I damn well can to make sure no more harm comes to her.

I give a brief rundown on the last few days, how I found Trish, the marks on her neck, and the story she told me about her ex. I leave out the warm feeling in my chest every time I see her with the baby, the way her smile makes my insides flutter, and the way the curve of her neck makes my dick hard.

But even so, there are knowing smirks around the table. Maybe I'm not as hard to read as I think I am.

"What do you need?" asks Prez.

He's not questioning me or my actions, and I'm thankful for my MC brothers' unconditional support.

"Club protection for Trish and Rose, the baby."

Vintage shifts in his chair. "Why don't you bring them in here to stay in the clubrooms?"

The thought of sharing Trish makes me tense. I like her in my cabin where I can keep an eye on her, where I can pretend she's mine.

I shake my head. "Too many people coming in and out, and she can't keep the baby quiet. Someone might get wind of her being here."

"Is her ex looking for her?" asks Badge. He's the Sheriff of Wild and handy to have in the MC.

"Dunno," I say. "He might be happy she's gone, or he might come looking for her."

"I'll ask my team to keep an eye out."

It's hard to track strangers on the mountain when we have tourists coming and going, but I appreciate his offer.

"She's Hailey's sister, right?" asks Hops. "When are they back?"

"No one can get ahold of them." I don't mention that I've stopped trying so hard. They might be back any day now, and my time with Trish is limited. I don't want to think about giving her up.

"But even when they're back, I want us to protect Trish."

Hops gives me a sideways smile. "You got a special interest in this woman?"

I pull at my beard and look down. I'm not ready to admit my feelings, not even to my MC brothers. But by the smirks on their faces, I can tell it's too late to hide.

"Yeah." It feels good to say it out loud. "Once I've dealt with this guy, she'll be my old lady. If she'll have me," I add.

Trish has been through a lot, and I'm not sure how she feels about me. Apart from the sweet kisses I planted on her neck yesterday, there's been no more intimacy. After what she's been through, I don't want to rush her, even though I'm aching to hold her.

There are broad smiles from around the table, and Hops slaps me on the back.

"Nice one, brother." He's grinning from ear to ear. "Love will change your life, I swear."

Barrels scowls at him. "Another pussy-whipped club member, that's all we need."

Vintage shakes his head at him. "You wait, brother. It'll happen to you one day too."

"Not likely," says Barrels. "I've got a brewery to run, and that's all I need."

Prez brings the meeting to order, and I leave the room while they vote. It's unanimous. The club will protect Trish and Rose like they're family. Relief settles over me knowing I have my brothers at my back.

The guys are staying for a drink, but there's only one place I want to be.

I'm about to leave when Prez calls me over. "I need you on the next run."

I nod and follow him to his office. It's the first time I've ever been reluctant to help with club business. But my brothers have my back, so I need to do my part.

Prez closes the door behind him, and we go over the details for the run.

8
TRISH

It's been two days since Joseph found me and took me in, and in those two days, the knot of anxiety I've carried around for so long has almost eased entirely.

It's easy to be here. Joseph left this morning for a club meeting and said he'd be home after lunch.

I've spent the morning wandering the trails near his cabin with Rose strapped to my front in the sling he bought me and bear spray in one hand. Rose had her little face turned up to the sunlight streaming through the trees, as in awe of this place as I am.

She's sleeping now in the travel crib we set up in the corner of the bedroom while I clean the kitchen. It's the least I can do for the man who has taken me in, cooked me meals, and bought supplies for my baby.

He must have lived here on his own for a long time,

and while the cabin appears tidy, I doubt it's ever had a deep clean.

I've pulled out all the supplies from the cupboard below the sink and I'm on my hands and knees with bright yellow cleaning gloves on.

There's a thick layer of grease, and my cloth leaves a clear path as I run through it. I sigh in satisfaction and wash the cloth out in the bucket of soapy water. Another few swipes and I've got the bottom of the cupboard back to a fresh white. I'm about to start on the cupboard door when the sound of tires crunching on gravel makes me start.

Joseph took his motorbike today, and this is definitely a car engine. My heart jumps into my throat, and I can't breathe.

How has Ian found me already?

I peer out from over the kitchen counter, and there's a huge car parked out the front of the house. It's some kind of classic old car with side wings. Not the type of car you find on the side of a mountain, but it's not Ian's beat up little Honda either.

A woman steps out of the passenger seat and she's as classic looking as the car, in a 1950s style dress with curves to match and her hair pinned up in a red scarf.

She pulls a bag out of the back and marches to the front door and knocks.

I'm frozen down on my knees, peering over the kitchen counter, not sure if I should answer it or not. I've got no idea who this strange woman is.

She shields her eyes and peers in as she knocks on the door.

"Hey," she calls. "I'm a friend of Lone Star. I've got baby clothes you can have."

At that moment Rose wakes up with a cry, and there's no point in pretending we're not here. I pop up from behind the kitchen counter and pull my gloves off.

"Just a minute."

I get Rose up before opening the door a crack.

The woman smiles when she sees Rose. "She's adorable."

Her eyes light up, and Rose smiles right back at her. "My little one's sleeping in the car; she'll be up soon."

I peer past her to where the car door hangs open, and there's the shape of a baby seat bundled up with a blanket.

"I'm Danni," the woman says. "My husband, Colter, is in the club. Thought you might need some baby things and a bit of company."

I like the woman instantly. She's got a friendly air about her. I'm about to invite her in when there's a cry from the car.

"Ah." She pauses. "Bettie's awake. It's always the same as soon as the car stops."

She retrieves her baby from the car and jostles her on her hip, soothing the tears.

"You mind if we come in for a bit? She needs a feed."

I make a bottle for Rose while Danni feeds Bettie. They're only a few months apart, and I chat easily with

Danni, sharing motherhood stories and baby tips. It's good to talk with another first time mom, and to meet one of Joseph's, or Lone Star as everyone seems to call him, friends.

While I pour Danni a coffee, I work up the courage to ask what I really want to know.

"What are the MC like?"

You hear bad stories about motorcycle clubs and what they're into, and I've only got Joseph's word to go on.

Danni nods knowingly. "They're good guys. They're not like the MCs you see on the TV."

She tells me about how her and Colter, known as Vintage, met and how the MC helped her set up her gallery and studio.

"It's like a family here. They'll do anything to help their own and protect them."

She eyes me intently, and I wonder how much Joseph has shared about my situation.

"He's a good guy, Lone Star. They call him that because he's always been a loner, but the star part is because he's loyal and true. You become his old lady, and he'll defend you to the ends of the earth."

I look down at her words, because I'm embarrassed it's that obvious what I'm thinking. That I want to stay here, that I want to hitch myself to his star and never let go.

"I've only known him for two days," I whisper, "but I don't want to leave." It feels good to confess it, to say it out loud.

Danni chuckles.

"The same thing happened to me. There's something about this mountain and the men on it. They both have a way of getting to your heart and not letting go."

Rose cries and Bettie wails in sympathy and we scoop them up, back to motherhood duties. Danni slings her baby bag over her shoulder as she holds Bettie on the other hip.

"I hope you stick around, Trish," she says before leaving. "I don't know your situation, but whatever it is, the club has your back."

As I watch her pull away in her beautiful but impractical car, the silence of the cabin settles around me.

I could get used to life here, to the peaceful quiet of the forest. And there's something else I'm feeling: a longing in my heart, an ache in my body. Joseph's been gone for half of the day, and I miss him. There's no denying it. I'm falling for the big, silent mountain man.

9
JOSEPH

The scent of cleaning fluid and fresh flowers hits me when I open the cabin door later that afternoon.

There's a vase of wildflowers on the center of the table, and the walls of the kitchen seem brighter. The windows are thrown open, the dust gone from around the window frames.

"You cleaned up?"

Trish is on the mat with Rose, the baby giggling as she dangles the colorful caterpillar over her head. My heart warms at the giggles coming from the both of them.

"I hope you don't mind."

I don't mind at all; I could get used to this. There's a feminine touch to the cabin now. The flowers and the open windows that are streak free bring the scent of the forest into my home.

Rose makes a crying noise, and Trish picks her up.

"I'm going to get her down for her afternoon nap."

She brushes past me, and I resist the urge to reach out and pull her toward me. I want to kiss her senseless. I thought about her all day, and I love coming home to her and the baby.

While Trish puts Rose down, I fix us a snack. Every cupboard has been cleaned, the walls wiped down and the taps polished so I can see my own bristly reflection in them. Damn, it's good having Trish around.

I fix us a bowl of guacamole and grab a packet of corn chips. Trish comes out of the room a few moments later.

"She asleep already?"

It usually takes a lot longer to get Rose down. She must be settling into the place.

Trish comes into the kitchen and picks up a dish cloth. There are a few items in the drying rack, and she gets busy putting them away. I love how we move around each other easily, like she belongs in the space. She's changed into a pair of short shorts, and I can't stop glancing at her luscious thick thighs.

"Danni stopped by today."

A pang of gratitude goes through me at my MC brothers and how quickly they've mobilized to help. Trish tells me about her day and the play date the babies had. I hope it can be a regular thing for her. I hope she'll stick around.

Trish reaches up to put a pasta bowl on the top shelf and my gaze goes to her legs, getting a peek of her upper thigh as she reaches up. My breath catches in my throat. There's an angry purple bruise at the top of her thigh.

"He hit you on the legs too?"

I stride across the kitchen and crouch down to examine the bruise.

Trish spins around in shock.

"I didn't know it was still there, sorry," she whispers.

The timidity of her voice makes my blood boil.

"Honey, you've got nothing to be sorry about. The man who did this to you is a monster."

She looks down, and I hate the red blush of shame that appears on her cheeks. I want to purge her of this asshole for good. Get all the pain out of her and make her brand new, as clean and fresh as my kitchen.

I stand up slowly.

"Is there anything else I need to know about, anything else he did to you?"

Her gaze meets mine, and she holds it for a long time. Pain flickers across her face, and I hate that someone made her feel that. That she has these memories.

"I'll show you."

She hooks her thumbs under her t-shirt, and I catch her hands.

"You don't have to show me if you don't want to."

We hold each other's gazes, and in that look, I recognize trust. "I want to show you. I want you to see all of who I am."

Her words floor me. And I'm speechless as she lifts her t-shirt over her head. I feel honored that this woman trusts me enough to bare her soul to me. I don't take that lightly.

Trish's body is amazing. Full heavy breasts and a curvy stomach. My breath hitches and my throat goes dry, but I'm not here for my own needs.

There are dark finger marks on her neck, and when she turns around, a bruise on her hip.

My blood heats. How could someone do this to a woman?

"Was this the first time?"

She shakes her head. "No, but it was the worst."

The marks are under her clothing, calculated. He probably learned this from his father, who learned it from his father before that. Generational domestic abuse that's somehow been normalized because that's all they've known.

My fists clench, thinking not just about Trish but the thousands of other women suffering in silence.

"Can I touch you?"

She nods, and I trace the marks from her neck to her hips and thighs. With every bruise my finger crosses, I make a silent vow to protect this woman with my life.

"No one will ever hurt you again, Trish. Ever."

Her eyes meet mine, and the vulnerability makes my heart break. This woman's been torn apart, and I'm going to put her back together.

I pull her into my arms. Her body is soft and tender against my large hard frame. I've never understood how a man can hurt a woman. They're smaller and softer, and we're supposed to protect them, keep them safe.

Her body molds to me, and there's a moment when the warm hug turns into something more. Her body presses against mine, and her hips move against me. My cock hardens and I step away, not wanting to add to her discomfort.

"Stay." She keeps her arms tight around me and pulls my hips toward her.

Her head tilts up, and I look down at her wide eyes. Her lips part, and we're both breathing hard. She's vulnerable. She's under my protection. I should walk away, give her space.

"Kiss me."

Her plea holds me in place. My heart thunders against my rib cage as I look down at the woman in my arms. The first person to penetrate my heart, my very soul.

She parts her lips, and there's need in her eyes.

"Are you sure?" My thumb grazes her cheek. "Because if I kiss you, there's no going back. This is for keeps, Trish. I want you as my woman, in my cabin. You and Rose."

Her eyes widen. It's a lot, I know that, but I've never been a man to do things by halves. I need her to understand that.

"I want that too." Her words stir something deep inside me, something warm and needy, a sense of belonging that I never knew I was missing.

My thumb brushes her lips, and she whimpers. I

wonder how long it's been since she was touched the way a woman should be touched.

My lips press to hers, and warmth spreads through my veins. It's a slow kiss, tender and gentle. There's a lot of healing that needs doing, and I won't give in to my animal instincts until she's ready. My hands slide down her back, tangling in her hair as I touch every part of her, needing to feel her skin against mine.

She tastes like coffee and baby milk, and it's my new favorite flavor.

Her hands hook under my t-shirt, and she pulls it over my head. Her hips grind against mine and my dick responds, pushing against my jeans until I think the seams will burst.

But this isn't about me. Trish needs to be shown love. She needs to be worshipped the way she deserves.

Her fingers pull at my belt buckle, but I stop them with my hands. She looks up at me, confused.

"I'm gonna give you what you deserve, Trish. I'm gonna show you how a man's supposed to treat a woman."

10

TRISH

*J*oseph sinks to his knees, his palms scraping over my thighs as he does. There is so much running through my head right now: Should I be doing this? What if Rose wakes up? When's the last time I shaved *down there*?

But all thoughts flee my brain when his warm breath caresses the skin of my thigh. I gasp at the sensation of his beard scratching against my delicate skin as his soft lips work their way up my thigh. He gets to the top of my shorts and yanks them down, exposing my threadbare cotton panties.

His hands caress the gusset, and his breath catches.

"You're already wet."

I've been wet for this man since he took me in. Kissing Joseph feels like a relief, confirmation that my feelings over the last few days are real, that he feels them too.

But as his fingers run between my legs and his breath hits my thighs, the warmth I felt at the kiss turns to pure pleasure. The knot in my stomach disappears completely, and a new sensation begins to build. A beautiful carefree sensation that I haven't felt in a long time. As his fingers slide under my panties, I feel like I'm floating, like I don't have to worry about anything. For this moment, it's all about me and my pleasure.

I barely notice Joseph peeling my panties off and slinging my leg over his shoulder. We're still in the kitchen, and I grab hold of the counter with one hand as his tongue licks my swollen folds. My thighs clench together, not used to having a man down there.

Joseph sits back on his haunches, his gaze on my pussy.

"You're beautiful, Trish."

No one's ever worshipped me down there like he is.

Joseph nudges my thighs apart and I open for him, feeling vulnerable but in safe hands. He dips his head with reverence and slowly kisses the most intimate parts of me. His tongue slides into my opening, and he groans at the same time I moan.

The fact that he's getting off on this as much as I am helps me relax. I lean back, letting him take care of me. Meaty hands grab my butt, and he pulls me onto his face. His beard tickles me between the legs as his tongue flicks over every part of me.

It's erotic and dirty, and I want so much more of him. Feeling bold, I grind my pussy into his face. Joseph responds by sliding a finger inside me. My pussy sucks in his digit as the pressure builds inside my walls.

I lean back, gripping the counter as my moans echo around the kitchen. He's devouring me like I'm his favorite dessert, and it feels so good I can't hold on much longer.

Then I'm over the edge. Stars burst in my vision, and I stifle a cry. Waves of pleasure wash over me, and my spirit soars. For the first time in months I'm truly free, my body taking something for itself.

As the orgasm subsides, Joseph presses his face to me once more. I grab his hair and move his head where I need it, riding his face with a new confidence. It doesn't take long for another orgasm to claim me. My pussy pulses on his tongue, and he licks my juices up hungrily.

Only when my body is exhausted does he let up.

He lowers my leg and stands up, wiping my juices off his beard.

I reach for the bulge in his jeans, wanting to return the favor, but he shakes his head.

"Tonight is all about you, Trish. Showing you how you deserve to be treated."

It's hard to believe his words. The only other man I've known is Ian, and he never did what Joseph just did. It's hard to believe there are men this good in the world, let alone that I've fallen for one.

My heart fills with gratitude and I push off the counter, but my legs buckle under me.

Joseph catches me in his arms.

"You must be exhausted."

He's not wrong. The exhaustion from the last several months has finally caught up with me. Living on the edge, never sleeping properly in case something happened to Rose. For the first time in months, I feel truly relaxed, and it makes my body heavy.

"Let's get you to bed."

Joseph leads me to the bedroom and I lean into him, feeling safe and satisfied.

"Stay with me tonight," I say, not wanting him to sleep on the couch.

"Trish, I'll spend every night with you for the rest of my life if you ask me to."

After checking Rose, I crawl into bed and Joseph wraps his arms around me. My body relaxes completely. I have him, and my daughter is safe. There is nothing to be anxious about. I fall into a deep, dreamless sleep.

11
JOSEPH

A mewling noise drags me from my slumber. The bed shifts next to me, and I smile as memories of last night fill my head. The taste of Trish's sweet pussy, the way she came, dancing on my tongue, and the release I gave her that she so desperately needed. And how we fell asleep, her warm body molded against mine like it was always meant to be there.

Rose's cries drag me from the memory, and I flick on the bedside light.

"Sorry," Trish whispers, "I'll take her out to the living room and change her."

She cradles Rose to her chest, but the baby doesn't stop crying.

"Don't apologize." I swing my legs over the side of the bed and catch her arm before she can scurry out.

"Change her here."

She kisses the top of Rose's head and rubs her back,

trying to calm her. I smile. I'll never get sick of the sight of the two of them in my cabin, even at five o'clock in the morning.

"Don't ever apologize," I say. "This is where you and Rose belong now, Trish. Don't apologize for the needs of your daughter."

She gives me a grateful look as she grabs the changing mat, and a flare of anger goes off inside me. That asshole ex of hers probably hated the baby crying. From what Trish has told me, he blamed her for Rose's crying instead of helping out with the baby like a parent should.

"I've got traps to check anyways."

Getting out in the woods will help with the rage I feel toward that scumbag. I've been neglecting my traps and haven't been hunting for the last few days. I need to get out to see if there are any animals I need to process.

Rose's cries have turned to giggles as she makes a grab for Trish's hair. Trish distracts her as she changes the diaper, shaking her head so her hair tickles Rose's face.

"She's wide awake now." Trish sighs. "I guess that's all the sleep I'm getting tonight."

But she's got a smile on her face, and who can blame her? Her daughter's giggles are infectious.

"You two climb back into bed. I'll fix you a bottle and a coffee."

"You don't need to do that, Joseph."

Trish efficiently puts the changing mat away all with

one hand cradling her daughter. She doesn't get it yet. She doesn't get that I'll do anything for her and the baby.

I slide my arm around her waist and pull them both toward me.

Rose looks up at me in surprise. Her little hand reaches out and grabs my beard. When she tugs on it, her eyes open wide in shock at the way it feels. Then she giggles and yanks on it again.

"You got some strength in you." I chuckle at the little girl. "You'll make a good hunter one day."

I've learned a few things about babies over the last few days, and it doesn't take me long to mix the formula and get the bottle heating. While the milk's warming, I put the coffee on.

It won't be light for another hour or so, but I love getting up in the predawn and getting out into the forest. Having a baby around the house suits me better than I ever thought it would. I'm used to early mornings.

When I go back to the bedroom, Trish is sitting up in bed singing nursery rhymes to Rose. I put the coffee down on the bedside table and hand her the bottle. Rose reaches for it greedily.

Before heading out, I stop at the bedroom door and spend a long moment watching them, Rose sucking hungrily while Trish sings softly to her daughter. My heart warms, and my chest expands. They're everything I never knew I needed in my life. And I hope to hell I can make them mine.

Frost crunches under my boots as I head into the forest. The well-worn paths crisscross in the undergrowth and today I take the east track, planning to circle around to check each of my traps.

When I came to Wild Heart Mountain, I bought this piece of land covered in forest. I know it intimately and I've come to love it, the wildlife, the trees, the weather patterns.

I'm already thinking about how I'll share it with Trish and Rose. The family walks I'll take them on. I'll teach Trish how to hunt and how to trap, how to live off the land.

My thoughts are flooded with the future as I come to the first trap.

There's a bunny in it, a big one that'll give us meat for the winter. I usually sell the pelts in town, but I'll make something for Rose out of this one, a blanket and some mittens to keep her warm for the winter that's coming.

Rabbit hide will make a good underlay for the crib, which I'll have to build. There are a couple of pines near the cabin where the wood will be perfect.

The cabin will need extending, but that can wait till the spring. I don't mind having Rose sleep with us for a few months.

We'll need a room for Rose and maybe more rooms for mine and Trish's kids.

The thought has me smiling. A few days ago, I would have run at the sight of a baby. But since meeting Trish, there's nothing I want more than to see my home filled with children. Our children. And I already count Rose among my own. I feel as responsible for her as I do for her mother.

With more mouths to feed and a bigger family, I'll have to hunt more. I'll extend the veggie garden, and we'll get a couple of chickens for fresh eggs. It'll be an adjustment, but my heart warms at the thought of Trish, belly round with a baby inside her, tending to the veggie patch.

It's a few hours later, and I'm on my way back with four bunnies strung over one shoulder and my hunting rifle over the other. There was no sign of deer today, but there's always tomorrow.

I'm whistling as I walk, thinking about insulating the cabin. With winter coming and a baby to take care of, I'll need to make some improvements.

I'm smiling to myself thinking about this new future as I come out of the thicket of trees near my cabin. I stop in my tracks.

There's a flicker of white through the trees, a car that I don't recognize. I drop to my knees and shrug the rabbits onto the ground.

My heart's racing, but my military training kicks in. Silently, I ease the rifle off my shoulder and move forward across the forest.

The car is a beat up Honda and not one that I recognize. I'll bet you anything that's her asshole ex.

I whip my phone out and make a quick call to Prez, thankful that I installed a satellite dish on the cabin.

I explain the situation to the Prez and tell him I'm going in. The MC will be here as soon as they can, but I don't know what's happening inside the cabin and I need to get to Trish and Rose.

Dumping everything but the hunting rifle, I creep closer to the cabin.

From what Trish has told me about Ian, he's the kind of guy who would bully a woman but shit his pants if he came up against anyone his own size. Well, he's going to get the scare of his life. I want him to see who Trish has in her corner now, that there's an entire MC protecting her.

But I have to be cautious. He's a man with a wounded ego. His girlfriend and baby left him. That must hurt, and there's no telling what he might do.

The front door is open a crack, and I push it all the way open with the barrel of my gun. Voices are coming from the bedroom mixed with the sound of Rose's cries. My heart hammers against my chest and I want to rush in there, but I've got surprise on my side. And as I learned in the military, surprise can go a long way in deciding an outcome.

I'm a big guy, but I can be stealthy when I need to. I creep through the cabin until I'm at the door of the bedroom. Keeping low to the ground, I edge the door open until I get a full picture of the situation.

A tall man with greasy hair holds Rose in front of him

as the baby screams and writhes in his arms. Her face is puckered, and her arms reach out for her momma.

"Just hand me Rose, please." Trish's eyes are wide and terrified, and I hate the desperation in her voice.

Her eyes are only on Rose, and she doesn't see me at first.

"Make her fucking stop, Trish. Tell her to stop fucking crying."

Ian jiggles the baby harder, making Rose scream.

"Give her to me and I'll make her stop, I promise." Trish reaches for Rose, but Ian holds her out of Trish's grasp.

My instinct is to shoot the fucker for what he's done, but he's holding Rose and she can't get hurt. I lower my gun and rise to my feet; I'll do this the old fashioned way.

This guy must be deaf as well as stupid, because he doesn't hear me sneak up behind him. Trish's eyes glance at me and I hold my finger out for her to be quiet, to not let him know I'm here.

I give her a nod, and we move at the same time. I barrel into Ian as Trish lunges forward and snatches Rose out of his hands.

Ian spins around just in time for my fist to connect with his face. He screams, which makes Rose scream louder.

"Get her out of here."

Trish cradles Rose to her chest and scoots past us out of the bedroom. As I lay into Ian, my vision goes red as all the rage simmering inside me comes out in my fists. I pummel the man who hurt the woman I love, and when he slumps to the floor, I kick him.

"You motherfucker."

Kick

"You think it's fun to hurt a woman."

Kick

"You're scum."

Kick

All the rage I've pent up since I saw Trish's bruise comes out of me. I've seen humans hurt each other. I've seen humans shoot each other and beat each other to death. In the military I learned how to fight and I learned how to kill. And that's where I go now. My years of training and the unofficial training I had from what I witnessed goes into each kick.

"Stop!"

Trish's voice cuts through my rage.

My foot pauses mid kick. Ian's in the fetal position on the floor, his arms covering his head as blood spurts from his nose. My boot is covered in his sticky blood, and there's an acrid smell from where he's pissed his pants.

I hate this man for what he did to Trish and Rose, but if I let my anger go and kill him, then I'm no better than him. I'm no better than the dehumanized soldiers from both sides who I witnessed doing bad things to each other.

But there is good in this world. I've witnessed it in the last few days, seeing Trish's devotion to her baby and the

MC coming together to help. Since I've lived on Wild Heart Mountain, I've only seen the good side of humanity. And maybe that's what humanity mostly is. Maybe what I witnessed was the exception.

If I take Ian's life, I'm no better than the dark side of humanity that I fear, but in the last few days I've seen the light. I've got something to live for now, an example to set for my family, for my daughter.

I stagger backward, breathing hard. Trish puts a hand on my shoulder and it's reassuring, her light in my darkness.

From out front comes the roar of bikes.

"You're not worth going to prison for." I grab Ian by his T-shirt and haul him to his feet.

He pleads with me not to hurt him as I shove him towards the door.

"There's nothing for you here, you understand? You lost your right to be with this woman and this baby."

He's blubbering, snot bubbling out of his nose mixed with blood. I almost feel sorry for him until he speaks.

"She took my money."

I'm so angry I almost hit him again. He loses a woman like Trish and his own baby, and all he can think about is the money that Trish took off him.

I pull a few bills out of my pocket and shove them at him. I don't want to give him any excuse to come back.

"Here's your money, asshole."

By this time we've reached the front door where Hops, Barrels, and Prez are getting off their bikes. The roar of engines coming up the path bring three more of my brothers.

Badge is absent, which is for the best. Plausible deniability if this loser is stupid enough to make a complaint.

If Ian was scared before, he's terrified now.

We're an impressive sight, my boys in leather patches with their big road bikes.

Trish comes onto the porch cradling Rose and the MC stand in front of her, forming a barrier.

Ian swivels his bleeding head between us with wide eyes, no doubt wondering what the fuck he's walked into. His gaze finds Trish and he looks vulnerable, like the schoolboy she must have fallen for.

"Come back, Trish," he says. "I miss you."

The fucker seems genuine, which pisses me off. How typical that he doesn't realize what he's got until he it's gone. I turn to Trish. There's no way in hell I'll let her go off with this scumbag, but he needs to hear it from her.

She steps forward, clutching Rose to her chest.

"It's over, Ian. Whatever we had. It's been over for a long time. I'm taking our daughter, and I never want to see you again."

Ian's face is a picture of agony. But I have no sympathy for this asshole. I shove him down the steps, and he staggers to his car.

I follow him, flanked by Barrels and Wood, until he gets into his shitty Honda. I'm proud to see Trish standing tall on the porch. Rose has stopped crying, and with my MC club flanking her, they look formidable.

Ian gets in his car and kicks up the gravel in a hurry to get out of here. Without being asked, Barrels and Wood get on their bikes and follow, giving him a personal escort off the mountain.

It's not till he's gone that my fists unclench.

I stride to my woman and put my hands on her shoulders, scanning her and Rose for any signs of harm.

"Are you okay?"

She's trembling but she juts her chin out, and I love how strong she is, not wanting to give him the power and setting a good example for her daughter.

"We're good. Thank you."

"I mean it, Trish. I want you to stay here with me. I don't want to be another man telling you what to do. But if you want it, there's a place for you here. You and Rose. I love you, Trish. And I'll protect you for the rest of my life."

Her bottom lip wobbles, and now the tears come. She buries her face in my chest, and I put my arm around her and Rose.

Prez catches my eye as he slips his phone into his pocket.

"Badge has got a team following the car to make sure it gets out of town. His plate will be on a watch list if he ever tries to get close again."

"He won't be that stupid."

I think about the kicking I gave him; how easy it would have been to keep going. But I didn't. I stopped. When it came to it, I was one of the good guys.

12
TRISH

My hands shake as I clutch Rose to my chest, her little heartbeat thundering against mine.

"It's okay." I rub her back, but I'm not sure if I'm soothing her or myself.

The relief at seeing Ian go makes my legs weak, and I cling to Joseph.

"Are you okay?" he asks.

It takes me a moment to answer. I think about Ian turning up, surprising us, and the fear that sliced through me when he took Rose. Then the relief when Joseph turned up.

I wasn't sorry to see Ian getting a beating, but I'm glad that it's over. He's a coward, and with the MC here he won't be back. Finally, I've got him out of my life.

"Do you need anything?"

I look up to the kindly face of one of the MC guys. I'm so relieved they turned up.

"We're fine. But do you want some coffee? Please, stay for breakfast."

I glance at Joseph, just realizing that I've offered his food up for everyone. I've gotten so comfortable here that it feels like my own home.

Joseph just smiles at me. "Yup," he says. "Least we can do is get you some breakfast."

I carry Rose inside and put her in the sling. She's wide awake, but I want to keep her close to me.

There's a carton of eggs in the cupboard and bacon in the fridge, and I get to work making breakfast for the men who showed up to help a stranger.

Joseph introduces me to his MC friends. They've all got two names. Travis has the road name Hops and works with Barrels, whose real name is Quentin.

Arlo's road name is Prince, as in Prince Charming. I can see why. He's younger than the others with a cheeky smile that he gives freely. He takes Rose off me, and she giggles as the big man throws her up in the air, charming my little girl. Colter introduces himself as the husband of Danni. He invites us over anytime we like for a play date.

There isn't enough room inside, so we take our breakfasts onto the porch and eat on the stairs.

Joseph takes Rose on his knee, and he puts a bit of runny egg on his finger. Her face screws up when she licks it, making the men laugh.

Everyone talks easily, and as I listen to the chatter of the men, my heart lifts. I feel safe here. It's a real family, and they've welcomed me with open arms.

A little while later, we wave off the last of the MC.

Rose is exhausted, and I give her a bottle and put her down for a nap.

When I come out of the bedroom, Joseph's on the porch, and I join him. We sit in companionable silence on the two rocking chairs, looking out at the forest and listening to the bird song.

He reaches across the chair and takes my hand.

"I meant everything I said, Trish. I want you here with the baby. I want to have our own babies with you. But it's got to be your decision."

It's not a hard decision. It's peaceful here, it's safe, and I've fallen for the quiet recluse with the kind heart. There's just one thing that's niggling at me.

"If you hadn't have found me on Hailey's doorstep, I don't know what I would have done."

He squeezes my hand. "There's no point thinking about that. That's not how it happened."

But he misunderstands what I'm getting at.

"I was lucky, Joseph. I had somewhere I could go. I had Hailey. But there are a lot of women with nowhere to go. Nowhere to run to."

An idea has been percolating in my mind for the last few days, but I don't know how to make it a reality.

"What if there was somewhere in the mountains, a refuge for woman and their children. Somewhere they knew they could escape to, no questions asked."

I'd hate for a woman to be in my situation and not be able to leave because she didn't know where to go.

Joseph looks at me thoughtfully. "Aren't there places like that already?"

"Yes. But not here."

I look out to the depths of the forest, the light that breaks through the clearing. "There's something healing about the mountains. They make you think. They connect you with nature and remind you there's a better life."

Joseph sits back in his chair and pulls on his beard. "The club's got some spare land near the compound. I could talk to the guys."

My heart leaps. I can't believe he's taking me seriously.

"It's all well and good, having a refuge in the mountains, but if it was run by a gang of burly ex-military bikers, you wouldn't get many assholes turning up looking for trouble."

My mouth drops open. I never thought about getting the MC involved, but he's right. What better protection than the Wild Riders MC?

My heart lifts with something I haven't felt in a long time, and it takes me a while to recognize it as hope. Hope for myself and hope for Rose, but also hope for other women in a bad situation that there might be something I could do to help.

"I love you."

The words slip out, and I clap my hand over my mouth. Joseph's eyes sparkle, and a rare smile spreads across his face.

"I love you too, honey."

He kisses me then, long and deep. I let out a sigh as our lips meet, and heat spreads through me.

Joseph pulls me out of my chair and onto his lap.

The baby's asleep, and we're outside. There's no one else here, just the forest, the birds and the breeze, the fresh air against my cheeks.

I wiggle my butt against him, feeling him harden under me. The heat between us is scorching as he kisses me hard.

Just then, my phone rings. I try to ignore it until I remember Hailey.

Jumping off Joseph, I grab my phone from inside.

"I just got your message. My god Trish, I'm so sorry."

She's frantic, and it takes me a while to calm her down and make her believe everything's all right.

I fill her in quickly about what happened, and she's horrified that she missed me until I tell her I've been staying with Joseph. It's awkward talking about him when he's right there, but I don't need to say much. My sister knows. She squeals with delight, and we make a promise to visit this afternoon.

I love my sister, but it's a relief to hang up the phone. Joseph's waiting for me with hungry eyes.

"Where were we?"

He sidles off the chair and sits on the porch steps and pulls me onto his lap, and this time I straddle him.

"I was about to make you my woman."

13
JOSEPH

Trish straddles me on the porch, her thighs scraping against my own. She gyrates slowly, pressing her hips into me and turning my cock to steel.

My hands run up her back and tangle in her hair, pulling her head back so I can kiss her neck. She moans at my touch as I nibble at the skin of her throat.

I've waited so long for this woman, and now she's mine. She's mine. For real and forever.

We fumble at each other's clothes, and I pull her T-shirt off her head. She pulls my shirt off, and the cool air dances across my chest.

I shuffle around so that I'm sitting with my feet on the first step and she's straddling me with her feet on the next step down, keeping her hips in a good position and giving me access to her pussy.

I unhook her bra, and her luscious tits pop free. My mouth moves over them, and I suck on her nipples one by one. The little whimpers that come out of her mouth drive me crazy.

"You can be loud out here, Trish. There's no one here but the trees and wildlife."

"You think the bunnies are watching?" She giggles, and it's the first carefree sound I've heard come out of her. I want to hear it again.

"Nah, not the bunnies. It's the deer that like to watch."

She laughs again and I capture her mouth, wanting to kiss that giggle and trap it forever inside me.

Her giggles turn to moans as I move my mouth down her throat and to her breasts.

My teeth scrape her nipple as I roll the other one around in my fingertips. Her hips buck at every movement, and her moans peak into little cries.

God, she's got sensitive nipples, and I fucking love that. I want to find every sensitive spot on her body and work it until she begs for mercy.

Her hands snake down my chest, fingertips running over every muscle and tangling in my chest hair. She tugs on it slightly and pricks of pain jolt through my body, making me gasp.

Her eyes go wide with delight at the discovery that she can get little noises out of me.

I love this exploration and I could explore her body all day, but right now there's something I need more.

I tug at her leggings, and she lifts her butt so I can slide her leggings and panties off. Then she's tugging at my jeans.

We stand up so we can dispose of our clothing, and when I sit back, it's on the porch.

She's standing before me naked, and my breath hitches. I can't breathe. She's a vision, this beautiful woman who came into my life, who's mine to keep, mine to protect. The bruising on her body has faded, and I swear to God, I will never let anyone harm her again.

"Come here, beautiful."

She moves forward slowly, shyly. I put my hands on her buttocks and breathe in the scent of arousal.

"Part your legs for me, honey."

She's standing above me, and she does as I ask. I look up into her eyes.

"I'm going to worship at your temple every day, Trish. You're beautiful, and you deserve to be worshipped."

I pull her butt towards me and slide her pussy onto my tongue, tipping my head back to get better access. I lean back and rest one hand on the porch as Trish shuffles forward. She grabs hold of the back of the rocking chair and spreads her legs wide for me. She's so fucking sexy, standing over me, her hips moving while she rides my tongue.

I've seen her confidence grow in the last few days. She's not the frightened mother I found. This woman I've got dancing on the end of my tongue is all confidence. I glance up as I move my tongue and appreciate the glorious sight of her tits bouncing above me.

Our eyes meet, and one hand slides down over her

breasts. Her thumb brushes her nipple, and her eyes roll backwards as she moans.

I fucking love it that she's playing with herself. While Trish works her tits, I bring my hand up and slide it between her folds, slipping a finger inside her pussy.

She's so fucking tight and wet. Her juices flow over my tongue and dribble into my beard.

I can't take it slow; I need to warm her up so that she's ready for my cock, which is hard as the wood I'm sitting on.

I lick and I suck, and I find her clit and flick it with my tongue as my finger pumps in and out of her.

"Joseph…" she moans, and I love the way she says my name.

I love the way that the breeze whips her hair, strands falling over her tits. There's bird song around us, and being outside with the forest surrounding us adds to my urgency.

"Joseph…"

Her voice is high pitched, and I can tell she's close.

I slide another finger inside and finger fuck her good while my tongue flicks her hard nub.

She's writhing on my face, hips jerking back and forth as she slides her pussy up and down my tongue.

"Joseph…"

She pants my name over and over, and it's the sweetest sound I've ever fucking heard.

Then her pussy convulses, and she's screaming my

name into the forest. Her juice explodes on my tongue and I lick it all up, not wasting a drop.

I don't even wait for her to stop trembling before I pull her down to me. She straddles my lap, and her eyes bulge at the sight of my ramrod straight cock aiming straight for her sweet spot.

"You ready for me, Trish?"

She nods, and that's all I need. Grabbing her hips, I pull her down hard, impaling her pussy on my aching cock.

As I sink into her, I let out a groan. Heat washes over me, and she feels so fucking good, so tight and wet that every nerve ending in my cock is standing on end.

Our eyes meet as I slide her slowly off my cock, then thrust her back down.

"Joseph..." She cries out, her eyes roll back in her head, and her fingernails dig into my shoulder. I jerk her up and down my shaft as her tits bounce in my face, loving the feeling of her hungry pussy squeezing my cock.

Her moans get high pitched again, and I rock her back and forth so her clit brushes against my body.

"I'm gonna come again."

Which is the sweetest thing I ever heard.

"Come for me, Trish, before I shoot my load inside you."

She whimpers. Then her pussy tightens, and she's screaming my name as the orgasm races through her.

My cock lengthens, and I thrust deep into her. My

cum shoots into her pussy in thick, hot ropes. As she screams my name, I let out a roar, bellowing into the woods like a rutting buck. Letting all the forest know that I claim this woman. Holding Trish close, I pump every last drop into her.

I've seen my woman with a baby, and now I want to see her pregnant. I want to see a baby in her belly and Rose in her arms.

We stay like that for a long time, panting and holding each other, naked on the cabin porch.

It's the cries of Rose that bring us apart.

But I don't begrudge her. I feel happy. I feel satisfied. I've got my woman; I've got a little family of my own. It's more than this loner ever thought he'd have.

EPILOGUE

TRISH

One year later...

Sweat sticks to my palms and I wipe them on my maternity leggings, hoping they don't leave a mark for the cameras.

Joseph puts a reassuring arm around my shoulder.

"You ready?"

His sparkling eyes are full of a confidence in me that I wish I felt. I let out a deep breath and pull my spine up as tall as my protruding belly will allow.

"Let's do this."

I step into the sunlight and falter when I see the line of cameras and waiting press. My gaze lifts behind them to the line of Wild Riders, their wives and Hailey. There are other people from the mountain who I recognize. The entire community has turned out for the opening of the center, and the support gives me courage and makes me stand taller.

I step confidently to the podium and waiting cameras. Joseph never leaves my side, glaring at anyone who gets too close.

He grumbled at me opening the center when I was eight months pregnant, but I reasoned it's better to get it up and running before the baby arrives. The center needs publicity, and I need to get the word out there to whoever needs to hear it.

The Wild Riders MC agreed to help fund the center. They leased me land near their compound and helped build the cabins that make up the retreat.

It's nestled in the woods, surrounded by a large fence and at least two Wild Riders on security at all times. The place really feels like a refuge.

The location is nondisclosed, which is why we're doing the press conference at the Wild Riders HQ. In the pamphlets and social ads, I give the same message. Go to the Hope train station and call the number I give out. We have volunteers on the mountain 24/7 ready to give a lift when a call comes in. Women and their children can stay as long as they need.

After the press conference, Hailey takes over, leading the press through to the bar, where there's a screening of a video we shot showing the facilities but being careful to hide any identifiable landmarks.

Maggie's done the catering, and Kendra helped plan the opening. I've got a team of mountain women who have helped me get this project off the ground, and I'm thankful for every one of them.

I'll join them inside soon for any further questions, but the hardest part of my day is over.

Danni has been watching Rose, who's an active one year old now. She hands her over to Joseph, and my daughter laughs as her father swings her into the air. He's the only father Rose will ever know, and that's fine by me. Ian didn't even try to get access to his daughter, not that I'd have let him. I haven't heard from him since he left the mountain. Badge made sure his team memorized Ian's license plate, and if he's stupid enough to set foot on the mountain again, he'll be notified.

Badge also took my statement and pictures of the bruises to keep on file in case I ever want to file a report.

I barely give Ian a second thought these days. I'm too busy. With our expanding family and the center to set up, it's been a hectic few months.

The knot in my stomach tightens, which is weird, because the press conference that I've been nervous about is out of the way.

My stomach clenches, and I gasp.

"What is it?" Joseph's at my side instantly, cradling Rose in his arms.

I look down to the puddle of water on the ground. His gaze follows mine.

"Oh shit."

I've never seen my husband look so terrified, and I bark out a laugh.

"Prez!" he shouts, and every member of the MC turns at his tone.

"I need a van and a driver."

He practically throws Rose at Danni as he lifts me into his arms. I'm already a curvy girl and when you add the baby in my belly, it's enough to make even Joseph stumble.

"I can walk."

I laugh as I bat his shoulder, but he won't put me down. It's useless to try to change his mind, so I relax in his arms as he carries me to the van that Prez has ordered into the courtyard.

"It's early. Why is it early?"

Joseph is seriously freaking out, and I try to explain that due dates are pretty random but he's too panicked. My laugh turns to a grimace as another contraction squeezes my insides.

Joseph practically throws me into the back of the van, and I just have time to buckle up before we take off. Luckily Arlo is driving and not my panicked husband.

Joseph's next to me in the backseat, and I grip his hand as another contraction washes over me.

"Breathe, honey, breathe." I hold his hand and do some breathing exercises, which he seems to need more than me.

The contractions are closer together than they should be, and I don't want to panic Joseph anymore but I have to ask.

"How long until we reach the hospital?"

"About thirty minutes," Arlo calls from the front seat.

The closest is the medical center in Hope, but I don't think we're going to make it in time. I cling on to Joseph as the contractions get closer together, and try to focus on the scenery as it speeds by.

As we bump down the mountain road and into Hope, I'm panting hard and ready to push.

I catch sight of Joseph's panicked face. I can't help giggling, even though I'm in pain and about to give birth in the back of a van.

"What you laughing at?" He looks at me like I'm crazy, and in this moment, I feel like I am.

"I hope you're ready to meet your daughter, because she's coming."

The last thing I see is Joseph's wide eyes. Then I'm pushing and panting, and a few moments later a screaming red bundle drops right into his lap.

We stare at the puckered red face in silence. Then the mouth opens, and an almighty scream comes from its lips.

Joseph holds up his new daughter. His panicked expression has turned to wonder.

My mountain man saved me when I was lost, and now I'm giving him the greatest gift I can give. A family.

* * *

WILD RUNAWAY BONUS SCENE

JOSEPH

Four years later...

"Hold it higher, sweetie, or you'll get the paws dirty."

Rose lifts her arms and hoists the bunny she's holding into the air.

It's almost as big as she is, but she won't let me carry it back. I've been taking Rose out trapping ever since she could walk, and this is the first time she's caught something herself.

"I'm gonna use the pelt to make a blanket for the twins," she says.

The proud smile hasn't left her face the entire walk back to the cabin.

"Or maybe I'll make a coat for Lily's doll."

The entire way home, she's been coming up with different ideas for what to do with the bunny. I like listening to her talk, my proud daughter.

The cabin comes into view between the trees, and Rose breaks into a run.

"Mommy, Mommy!"

Birds fly out of the trees and small animals scurry away in the undergrowth as she races past.

The cabin juts out into the clearing with the extension at the back and the second story. But with our growing family I'm beginning to wonder if it will be big enough.

At the sound of Rose's shouts, the door bangs open and Lily, her younger sister, hurries out. She's followed by the twins on their unsteady legs wanting to know what all the fuss is about.

And last of all Trish, my wife, follows them onto the deck, her blonde hair falling over her face. No matter how many fancy clips I buy her, the golden tendrils manage to escape somehow.

She's looking good, her body as curvy as when I first met her. Her eyes are glowing, with no sign of the fear that haunted her when we first met.

Lily gives a squeal when she sees the rabbit. My four-year-old daughter hasn't shown an interest in trapping like her older sister, which is fine. I kept waiting for a son to pass on my forest knowledge to, but with four daughters, I realize that may never happen. Rose loves the forest and has a keen eye for hunting. Lily loves animals too much. She'd rather pat the bunnies than trap them.

Which is why our place looks more and more like a zoo each day. Along with the chickens and goats, we've got bunnies, cats, a dog, and a wild fox cub that keeps hanging around and that I'm sure Lily's feeding.

"Dadda." Violet, one of the twins, stretches out her arms as I come up the stairs. She's my daddy's girl, and she squeals as I hoist her over my shoulder.

"I've got breakfast ready." Trish kisses me on the cheek, and I catch a whiff of her chamomile shampoo. She goes to move away, and I grab her around the waist.

"Not so fast."

Her eyes sparkle as I pull her back toward me and kiss her mouth. Our bodies collide, and I feel the familiar stirring whenever I touch my wife.

I'm thinking of all the ways I want to take her when a warm body squeezes between us.

"Momma." Iris reaches up her little hands, looking anxiously at Trish.

She's a momma's girl that one, following Trish around everywhere and getting jealous if I take too much of Trish's attention.

Trish lifts Iris onto her hip, and I slide Violet off my shoulder and onto mine. The twins reach for each other and I nuzzle into them, making them giggle with my bristly whiskers.

"Hey," shouts Lily, not wanting to be left out. She dances around our legs, wanting to be picked up. The twins start squealing, and Rose slings her rabbit down on the outside table and dances around with her sister.

It's noisy and chaotic, and I join in the laughter. Trish hands me Iris, and I twirl my twins around while the older girls try to catch me.

I catch Trish's eye, and she's beaming at us. We'll have our adult time later, once the kids are in bed. But for now, my girls have got my full attention.

I sink onto my knees, and four sets of little arms and legs climb onto me. I buck like a wounded animal and they squeal with delight, trying to stay on my back.

It's noisy, it's chaotic, and it's everything this reclusive mountain man never knew he needed.

* * *

WILD CURVES

A fake relationship for a weekend between a biker who wants more and a shy girl who can't give him the one thing he craves...

Mom's coming to visit, and she expects to meet my new boyfriend. Spoiler alert: I don't have a boyfriend. I pretended I had one to get Mom off my back. I didn't expect her to show up on the mountain to meet him.

In steps Arlo, the bearded, tattooed biker I've been crushing on since I started working at the Wild Riders MC HQ. We'll pretend to be together to keep Mom happy. But as the weekend goes on, I'm falling for the easy-going ex-military biker.

But there's a reason why I don't date, and not even Arlo can change my mind.

WILD CURVES

Wild Curves is a fake relationship romance featuring an ex-military mountain man biker and the shy girl whose curves he can't get enough of.

CHAPTER ONE

Maggie

My hand shakes as I place the plate of chocolate-coated strawberries on the bar counter.

Arlo gives me an encouraging look that makes my insides flutter. I look away quickly, hoping he thinks my nerves are because of the dessert I'm presenting and not the fact that his luminous smile is turned on me.

"Let's give them a taste."

My attention snaps to Travis as he snags one of the strawberries and stuffs it in his mouth. He's the boss of the Wild Taste Bar and Restaurant and the person I have to impress if I want to get the pastry chef position once Patrick retires at the end of the year.

I hold my breath as he chews. His brows knit together and then raise in surprise.

"There's chili in these?"

CHAPTER ONE

I nod. "A little, to offset the sweetness."

"Mmmm…" Travis nods appreciatively. "These are good." He reaches for another one, and Kendra slaps his hand out of the way.

"Leave some for the rest of us."

She's the only one who can get away with playfully slapping the boss. He picks one up anyway and brings it to her lips.

Kendra opens her mouth to receive the strawberry and Travis pulls it away, just out of her reach. They both giggle and I look away, my ears turning pink at the intimacy of the moment.

Arlo catches my gaze and rolls his eyes heavenwards, making me smile. He works the bar and makes no secret of how sick he is of seeing Kendra and Travis all over each other since they got together.

I think it's sweet, the boss and the head waitress.

"What did you say these are called?" Arlo asks.

The blush spreads up my neck, and heat blooms in my cheeks.

"They're um… Strawberry Sin."

Arlo's eyes go wide, and a smile curls up his lips. "They taste like sin too."

As he says it he bites into the strawberry, breaking the chocolate seal with his teeth. My eyes dart to his lips. Lips so full they look indecent on a man. Lips so full they haunt my dreams as I imagine what they taste like, strawberry and chocolate with a hint of chili and cardamom. Sweetness and heat and something manly and exotic, which was my inspiration for the dessert. My knees go weak and my blush deepens.

"I need to get back to the kitchen and clean up."

I scurry away before the sight of Arlo enjoying the dessert that he was the inspiration for causes me to melt right onto the restaurant floor.

When I'm safely back in the kitchen, I lean so my forearms rest on the silver bench and let the coolness of the metal calm my heated skin.

All bartenders are terrible flirts, I tell myself. He likes my desserts and that's all.

Through the round window of the swinging kitchen door that leads to the restaurant, I watch as my three colleagues enjoy the rest of my strawberry sins.

I've been working at the Wild Taste for three months now, and any normal person would be out there chatting and laughing with their colleagues. The last customer left a half hour ago, and while they've been out there enjoying their drinks, I asked if I could present Travis with a dessert I've been working on.

I should be out there socializing, but I prefer the cool steadiness of the kitchen. Especially after hours when everyone else has gone home.

My phone rings, and I stifle a groan when I see it's Mom calling.

I contemplate slipping it back in my pocket, but I've already missed two calls from her today. She'll get frantic if I don't pick up.

"Hi Mom."

CHAPTER ONE

"Maggie!" She screeches so loud that I pull the phone away from my ear. "I couldn't get hold of you."

"I'm working, Mom. Didn't you get my text?"

"You know I find it hard to read those things. Call me old-fashioned, but I prefer to talk."

Old-fashioned is definitely the word I'd use to describe my mother. And if this call is anything like the daily calls I get, I brace myself for what I'm in for.

"You work too hard, sweetheart. Make sure you leave time for yourself to have some fun."

I lick a bit of chocolate off my hand and try not to roll my eyes.

"Working is fun for me. I've invented a new dessert."

I try to sound upbeat, but as usual Mom pays zero interest to my professional life.

"You'll never meet anyone if you're working all the time, MeMe."

She uses my pet name from childhood and the stern but kindly tone that my mother has perfected.

It's incomprehensible to my mother that I would put my career ahead of meeting a suitable husband. This is usually where I tell her I don't want to meet anyone, and she gasps like she's having a heart attack. But I can't do it today.

We've had this same conversation for the last two years, since I went to culinary school and told her I wanted to be a pastry chef.

"And your uterus isn't getting any younger, sweetheart. Fertility starts to decline after thirty, you know."

The last is said in a whisper as if someone might hear her down the phone lines.

"Mom, that's not really true…"

"It is," she protests. "I read it in a magazine. These women putting their careers first…"

She launches into a tirade spoken in hushed but disapproving tones about 'these women' when what she really means is me.

"Mom…" I try to cut in to remind her that I'm only twenty-three, but as always, I'm no match for my mother once she gets on a roll.

It's been a week of early double shifts, and the tiredness behind my eyes shifts to a full blown headache as I listen to my mom drone on. I press my fingers to my forehead and close my eyes, knowing from experience that it's best to let her run on until she's finished.

I love my mother, but it's the same lecture every week. Her first reaction when I told her I wanted to be a chef was how difficult the odd hours would be for raising a family.

I hadn't thought about that aspect of working life before. I just wanted to choose a career doing something I loved. Mom brings it up so often that I guess it's true.

As Mom drones on about the declining health of my ovaries, I watch Arlo through the window. He's chatting easily with Travis and Kendra, and a pang of longing jolts my insides. I shake it off. Mom's made it abundantly clear to me that if I want to be a pastry chef I'll never have a family. That's why I don't date. Even if the ridicu-

CHAPTER ONE

lously handsome and charming bartender had an interest in small, tubby shy girls, there wouldn't be any point in dating him.

My head aches, and I want to get off this call with Mom and find out what they really thought of my dessert and if Travis will put it on the menu. If only there was a way to get Mom off my back once and for all.

"I want a promise from you that you'll go out and make an effort to meet someone."

My mom doesn't get it at all. There's a reason I took a job in the middle of a mountain. Here, I can focus on my career with no distractions. There's a bar in Wild that I've been to with Kendra once when she dragged me out. But hanging out with strangers is not my thing.

"Put on a short skirt, sweetheart. Don't be afraid of those thighs you inherited from me. Some men love chunky girls. Look at your dad!"

She cackles like we've shared a secret, and my belly churns as I try not to think about my dad checking out my mom's thighs. Never mind the reference to my short stumpy legs. I'm immune to Mom's thoughtless comments by now.

When I'm not experimenting with new dessert recipes or thinking about new dessert recipes, I'm watching cooking shows and, on my days off, visiting every restaurant and cafe in the area to see what they've got on the menu. I may be shy, but I'm focused and determined. And I will not promise my mom that I'll go to a bar to look for men.

CHAPTER ONE

"I'm not going out to a bar, Mom."

"Oh honey..."

There's disappointment in her voice and she takes a deep breath, but before she can start the next lecture, I jump in.

"I already met someone."

I clamp my mouth shut as soon as I say the words. There's silence on the other end of the line.

"Say that again?"

"I...uh... met someone." I swallow hard, hoping she doesn't hear the lie in my voice.

"You've met a boy?"

"Ya-ha." My palms start to sweat. I've never been a good liar, and Mom is suspicious as hell.

"Are you going steady? Is he your boyfriend?"

My eyes go to Arlo leaning casually against the bar, a smile peeping out from his thick beard. "Yup. I got me a boyfriend."

"Oh MeMe. That's fantastic," my mother gushes. I wish she'd been this happy when I told her I got into culinary school or when I won the creative dessert award.

"What's he look like? Is he hunky?"

"Umm..." My gazes slides over Arlo, and I take a step closer to the door so I can see all of him through the small round window. His head is tilted back in a laugh, the deep rumble of his chuckle reaching me through the kitchen door and doing weird things to my belly.

"Um, he's tall and he's got a beard."

285

CHAPTER ONE

"A beard!" Mom exclaims. "I guess that's what you young folk are all into. But I wouldn't have looked twice at your father if he had a beard. What's his name."

"Arl…" I start to say and snap my mouth shut just in time. My fantasy almost got away from me, but I'm not giving out Arlo's name to my mother. She'd probably look him up online.

"What's that honey?"

"Allan." I wince.

"Allan? Not a very romantic name, but you can't help that. Where did you meet him?"

"Umm…" My brain freezes and I regret even starting this lie, but I'm in too deep to back out now. The best lies have a grain of truth, so I decide to stick to some semblance of realness. Besides, she'll never know. "He works at the restaurant."

"He's not a chef, is he? Unsociable hours. It'll hard when you have a family."

"Mom…"

"Oh, I know, honey, I'm just so excited. Thinking about my grandbabies. Jim!"

She calls out to my dad, making me wince and wondering if I've just given her more fuel for the grandbaby pressure.

"Jim! MeMe's got a boyfriend!"

Dad mumbles something in the background. I don't know how my softspoken dad puts up with my mother. I've never met two such different people. Mom's loud and talks non-stop, while Dad's quiet and observant. I know which one I take after.

"We'll come visit this weekend and meet Allan."

Wait, what?

My attention snaps back to my mother. "You don't have to do that."

"Of course we do. My little girl's got her first boyfriend. We have to meet this Allan and see if he's good enough for you."

Oh shit.

My palms sweat, and panic sets in.

"Um, we're both working this weekend. Double shifts."

"That's alright, honey. We'll look around the mountains. We've been meaning to visit and see the place. There's some good shopping in Hope, I hear. Hey, does Allan fish? Should Dad bring his rod?"

Oh my god, this got out of control real fast. My palm goes to my forehead as I try to backtrack.

"Um, I don't know. Please don't come. It's too soon…"

But as usual Mom barrels over me.

"We've been meaning to come and check out the Wild Taste Restaurant. Dad's worried that it's run by a MC."

"But…" I try to protest that the Wild Riders are ex-military and not into anything sketchy, but Mom cuts me off.

"Oh, I know what you're going to say, but your dad wants to check it out for himself. See what the club that employs you is all about."

CHAPTER ONE

I stride to the kitchen door and peer out through the round window. Arlo sees me and holds up the last strawberry.

"It's good," he mouths, and my stomach does a little flip.

"I gotta go," says Mom. "We'll see you Friday, MeMe. You and Allan."

I press my head against the door and close my eyes.

What have I done?

Read Wild Curves at mybook.to/WRMCWildCurves

* * *

GET YOUR FREE BOOKS

Sign up to the Sadie King mailing list and you'll get four FREE steamy romance books and access to all the bonus scenes!

You'll be the first to hear about new releases, exclusive offers, bonus content and all my news. You can even email me back. I love chatting with my readers!

To claim your free books visit:
www.authorsadieking.com/bonus-scenes

BOOKS BY SADIE KING

Wild Heart Mountain

Military Heroes

Mountain Heroes

Wild Riders MC

Temptation

Sunset Coast

Underground Crows MC

Sunset Security

Men of the Sea

Love and Obsession (The Cod Cove Trilogy)

His Christmas Obsession (Christmas)

Maple Springs

Men of Maple Mountain

All the Single Dads

Candy's Café

Small Town Sisters

For a full list of titles check out the Sadie King website

www.authorsadieking.com

ABOUT THE AUTHOR

Sadie King is a USA Today Best Selling Author of over 100 short contemporary romance.

She lives in New Zealand with her ex-military husband and raucous young son.

When she's not writing she loves catching waves with her son, running along the beach, and good wine, preferably drunk with a book in hand.

Sign up to her newsletter to receive all the latest news and releases and access to exclusive bonus content.

Sign up at www.authorsadieking.com/bonus-scenes

www.authorsadieking.com

Printed in Great Britain
by Amazon